D0871975

THE BALLOON BOY
OF
SAN FRANCISCO

The Balloon Boy
of San Francisco

by

Dorothy Kupcha Leland

Tomato Enterprises
Davis, California

The Balloon Boy of San Francisco
by Dorothy Kupcha Leland

Tomato Enterprises
P.O. Box 73892, Davis, CA 95617
(530) 750-1832   www.tomatoenterprises.com
info@tomatoenterprises.com

Library of Congress Control Number: 2004095368
©2005 Dorothy Kupcha Leland
Cover and map by Jan Adkins
First edition
Printed in the United States of America

Publisher's Cataloging-in-Publication
(Provided by Quality Books, Inc.)
Leland, Dorothy Kupcha.
    The balloon boy of San Francisco / by Dorothy Kupcha
Leland.   p. cm.
    Includes bibliographical references.
    SUMMARY : In 1853, a San Francisco newspaper boy struggles to support his family. An encounter with a hot-air balloon brings adventure and opportunity.
    ISBN 0-9617357-4-0
    ISBN 0-9617357-9-1 (paper)

    1. Gates, Ready—Juvenile fiction. 2. Ballooning—Juvenile fiction. 3. Hot air balloons—Juvenile Fiction. [1. Gates, Ready—Fiction. 2. Ballooning—Fiction. 3. Hot air balloons—Fiction.] I. Title.

PZ7.L53732Bal2005   [Fic]
                            QBI04-800004

Local author 8/06 PMR

The Path of Ready's Balloon Ride

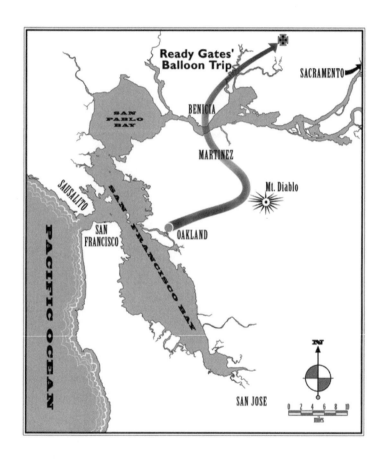

To Bob, Jeremy, and Rachel,
who buoy up my spirits.

This historical novel is based on a true story. Ready Gates really was a newsboy in Gold Rush-era San Francisco, and the major news events portrayed really happened. Some situations have been fictionalized.

CHAPTER ONE

Fog shrouded San Francisco early Thursday as Ready raced towards the center of town. The oil street lamps did little to light his way, but Ready never faltered along the wood-planked roadway. Though not yet six o'clock, the streets near Portsmouth Square were already crowded with horses, wagons, and pushcarts. Ready dodged them expertly as he ran pell-mell towards the office of the *Daily Alta California*. An editor, Mr. Garfield, met him at the entrance.

Ready leaned against the doorframe, gasping for breath. "John said to come immediately. The *Independence* is lost?"

Mr. Garfield nodded. "Wrecked off the coast of Lower California. At least one hundred and twenty-five dead."

"*Let's go!*" interrupted a loud voice. "Get these out on the street *now.*"

Ready grabbed a stack of papers emblazoned with the words, "EXTRA—March 31, 1853." As he headed out the door, two more panting newsboys arrived. Ready couldn't contain a smile. Once again, he'd gotten there first. Charles would have a hard time topping that.

He shouted into the foggy darkness. "TOTAL LOSS OF STEAMSHIP *INDEPENDENCE!* MORE THAN 125 PEOPLE DEAD."

A man unloading a wagon dropped a crate in the street. "Redhead! What did you say?"

"*Independence* shipwrecked, sir."

The man's face went white. "I was expecting my brother on the *Independence*," he whispered. Snatching a paper, he thrust a coin at Ready.

Another man appeared. "What's this about the *Independence?*"

By the time he reached the corner of Montgomery and Clay, Ready was surrounded by a crowd. Whenever his supply of papers ran low, someone brought another stack.

"Keep going, Red! I'll bring you more as you need them."

For hours, Ready stood at that corner, while the parade of people kept coming. Businessmen. Workmen. Society matrons. People in foreign-looking clothes, with foreign accents. Everyone asked: *What happened to the Independence?*

At noon, Ready wandered wearily back to the *Alta* office.

"Good show, Red," Mr. Garfield said. "You did a great job getting that paper out. I hope your brother can do as well."

"He'll do fine, sir," Ready replied. "What's the latest on the shipwreck?"

"The *Meteor* is bringing in the survivors," Mr. Garfield said. "It's a whaling ship. Should arrive this afternoon."

"How did we hear about it?"

"The *Meteor* was becalmed yesterday afternoon, about fifteen miles outside the Golden Gate. The captain of the

Independence and some of his crew rowed ashore in one of the small whaling boats. They reached port at midnight."

"What now?"

"Our reporter has taken a boat out to meet the ship. If the wind keeps up, the *Meteor* should be here this afternoon."

Ready took some money from his pouch. He counted out ten cents for each paper he'd sold and paid it to Mr. Garfield. Then he ran home.

To Ready's surprise, the house was empty. His father and the boarders were at work, of course, and his younger brothers in school. But why wasn't his mother sewing in the parlor? That order for six dozen pew cushions was due at the Congregational Church in two weeks. He shrugged and went upstairs to the bedroom he shared with his brothers.

Luckily, soon Ready wouldn't have to worry about silly pew cushions any more. Charles would take over more than Ready's newspaper job. He'd also have to help Mother measure and cut green velvet. Yards and yards of it! Ready grinned at the thought. Charles would hate it. Well, that was his brother's problem. He and Father had bigger fish to fry.

Ready dumped his money on the bed and counted it. *$84.25*. More than he'd ever earned at one time before. He counted it again. $84.25.

Next, he pulled a faded carpetbag from under the bed. For the hundredth time that week, he checked its contents. A wool blanket. Clothes. A tin cup and plate. Eating utensils. And best of all, a small, battered crevicing spoon to pry gold from the spaces between rocks. A sailor on the *S.S. Lewis* had given it to him months before, for good luck. Finally, he'd get to use it! Ready shoved the bag back under the bed and went downstairs.

Since today was Steamer Day—the day before the mail ship sailed—his mother had left a letter to Grandma on the kitchen table. Ready put it in his pocket. Charles would take over mailing letters, too. His brother shouldn't mind that. Ready put an orange in his pocket, for later. Then he wandered into the parlor.

Stacks of green velvet pew cushions filled the room. Bolts of material sat on a table, with scissors, thread and a pin cushion. Ready felt a twinge of guilt for abandoning Mother in the middle of this big project. But only a twinge. Besides, Ready would make it up to her. After he and Father struck pay dirt, they'd buy her one of those newfangled sewing machines he'd read about in the *Golden Era*.

A framed daguerreotype of his grandmother hung over the fireplace. The image of that stern wrinkled face brought back the memory of her last-minute words to him: *"Stay in school. Don't gamble. Don't let alcohol pass your lips. Take care of your little brothers."* Her voice had caught in a sob. *"And hurry back home."*

"Well, Grandma," Ready now answered the likeness on the wall. "San Francisco schools don't go past eighth grade. When I played cards at the El Dorado, I lost my money. I tried whiskey and didn't like it. And my brothers want me to leave them alone." As for returning to Philadelphia, well, that would happen in due time. After he and Father made their pile.

The post office was eerily subdued for Steamer Day.

"My landlady's nephew was due on that ship," a man in front of Ready murmured to another. "She's been worried sick about him for weeks."

Behind him, another man spoke quietly. "And so soon after the sinking of the *Tennessee*. The steamship companies will answer for *this*."

A woman walking back from the ladies' window whispered to her companion, "I don't want to set foot on a ship ever again."

After mailing his letter, Ready hurried to Long Wharf. Usually, crowds greeting ships were raucous and rowdy. Not today. A somber group watched the whaling ship drop anchor out in the bay. Several taxi boats rowed out to bring the survivors ashore.

First to scramble from the rowboats was a scrawny young man with wild hair and torn clothes. He stood on the dock for a moment and then fell to his knees and kissed the wharf's dirty planks. The crowd burst into spontaneous cheers and applause. It broke the tension. People came forward to help the others out of the boats.

Ready studied the dismal parade of people before him. There were mostly men with tattered clothes and bare feet. They stumbled down the wharf in a daze, not looking at anyone.

But one of the passengers stood out from the others. A tall teenaged girl wearing faded rags and men's heavy boots. Beneath a thatch of tangled hair, her eyes darted frantically, as if scouring the crowd for a familiar face.

As she walked past him, the girl tripped on an uneven board and let out a startled cry. Ready caught her arm.

13

Steadying herself, she mumbled, "Thank you, boy. I'm having some trouble with these shoes."

Ready cringed as she called him "boy," hating anew how people always mistook him for being much younger than his fourteen years. But the anguish he saw on the girl's face made him want to help her. What could he do?

As she moved away, he called after her. "Miss, wait!" He handed her the orange from his pocket. "Take this."

She stared at the orange as if unsure what it was. "Thank you," she murmured. Then she headed down the pier, still anxiously examining every face she passed.

CHAPTER TWO

Early the next morning, Ready threaded his way through the foggy streets to the waterfront. Express company wagons vied for space with produce carts, flower sellers, and people carrying luggage and parcels of all shapes and sizes. Three side-wheel steamers were scheduled to depart that morning. Ready expected another good sales day. Not as good as yesterday, of course. But enough to make his last week in San Francisco a profitable one.

"*ALTA CALIFORNIA,*" Ready called as he walked. "LIST OF SHIPWRECK PASSENGERS SAVED AND LOST."

A man stepped from a horse-drawn omnibus, holding a carpetbag and a basket of fruit. "Over here, newsboy."

Behind Ready, came another voice. "Redhead. Here. You have the names?"

Ready passed by the mail steamer *California* preparing for departure to Panama. Grandma's letter would be in its hold. With luck, she'd have it in her hand in five or six weeks. By then, Ready and his father would be long gone from San Francisco.

"*ALTA CALIFORNIA.* LIST OF SHIPWRECK PASSENGERS SAVED AND LOST."

15

"Over here, boy."

There was still so much to do. Father would work at the brick factory, and Ready would sell newspapers for exactly one more week. Then, leaving Mother, Charles, and Hugh to carry on without them, the two would travel by boat and then by stagecoach to Mariposa County. There, they would join Marcus Seldon, a family friend who'd built a one-room log cabin on the banks of Agua Fria Creek. All spring and summer, the three would work that creek bed for gold.

"ALTA CALIFORNIA."

When Ready reached the *Sierra Nevada,* boarding passengers for Nicaragua, he hurried up the gangplank. He spotted a cluster of men sharing a farewell nip from a pocket flask. *"Alta California?"* Ready asked. "They make great souvenirs back home."

His papers sold quickly, mostly to Americans returning east. But foreigners bought them, too, probably as keepsakes. Pressing himself through the crowded passageways, Ready heard snippets of Spanish, Swedish, and German, as well as a language he didn't recognize. He glanced at the speaker's swarthy skin. Arabic, maybe?

Ready went below deck to the ship's saloon. *"Alta California?* Take a bit of San Francisco to the folks back home."

He was startled by a voice. *"Ready Gates.* As I live and breathe!"

Whirling quickly, Ready found himself looking at Matthew Conway, the older brother of a school chum from Philadelphia. "I didn't do it," Ready said, putting up his hands in mock surrender. "Whatever they say I did, I didn't do it!"

Matthew threw back his head and laughed. "Knowing you and my little brother, you not only did it, you found a way to make money at it."

"You and your friends left for California the year before we did, Matthew. Are you going home?" Ready's voice dropped to a conspiratorial whisper. "*Did you make your pile?*"

Matthew shook his head ruefully. "I piled up more experience than gold dust, I'm afraid. I've got a *grand pile* of experience and not much else."

"What about your friends?"

Matthew grimaced. "Tommy Warren died from Yellow Fever crossing the Isthmus. Martin Kroger and I continued on to San Francisco, and then to Placerville. Last spring and summer, we found just enough gold to keep ourselves in food and shelter. This past winter was miserable. Martin wants to try his luck in Oregon, but I'm going home."

The smile returned to Matthew's face. "Did your whole family come west? Even the little tykes?"

Ready nodded. "They're not so little anymore."

"How long have you been here?"

"Since October. The weather was too bad to travel to the gold country, so we stayed here. But next week, Father and I leave for Mariposa."

"If you have a paying job," Matthew said, "you're better off in San Francisco."

The ship's horn sounded a warning blast.

"That's my signal to leave the boat," Ready said, handing Matthew a newspaper. "Give your family this *Alta California*. Tell them someday they'll read about how rich and successful I've become."

Matthew clapped a hand on Ready's shoulder. "Best of luck to you, my friend."

With a wave to Matthew, Ready left the *Sierra Nevada*. As he stood on the pier, a last-minute passenger came running down the wharf shouting, "Wait for me!" The man raced by, snatched the newspapers from Ready's hands and bolted onto the ship. Before Ready could react, the sailors removed the gangplank.

"Thief!" Ready shouted angrily after him.

Then, the paper-snatcher called down to Ready from the ship's railing. "Newsboy. Catch!"

Ready stretched out his arm and caught what the man threw him. A twenty-dollar gold piece! He grinned up at the man and saluted. Then he turned on his heel and headed back to town.

CHAPTER THREE

The departure of the three steamers did nothing to quiet the frenzied activity at the waterfront. The clipper ship *George Raynes* arrived with nine hundred tons of pond ice from Boston. The *Sansonette* brought two hundred women and children from France. Along with tea and silks, the *Mary Adams* delivered a hundred Chinese men. The newcomers shuffled down the wharf in single file, wearing dark clothing and wooden shoes. The first time Ready had seen men like this, everything about them had seemed peculiar and mysterious. Their long black hair pulled tightly into pigtails, their dark skin and slanted eyes, the strange sounds of their language. But now, he barely noted their presence.

Ready walked briskly to Winn's Fountainhead. Now that his mother spent most of her time sewing, she no longer baked six loaves of bread each day. Instead, Ready bought them at Winn's. Another job for Charles after next week.

As he stood in line for bread, Ready thought about Matthew Conway. Hard to believe a fellow would come all the way to California and then leave without making his pile. If Matthew couldn't find gold in Placerville, well, he should have tried someplace else. According to the *Alta California*, a nugget worth almost four thousand dollars had been found near Sonora last week. You just had to look in the right place!

Ready bought the bread and headed home. Matthew's hard luck story didn't scare him. If anything, it made him more determined. He hurried by the post office, deep in thought.

"Ready Gates!" He looked up to see his friend Max Sweeney waving a small tin disk. "How about a last game of buzzers before you're too high-falutin' to keep company with the likes of us?"

Grinning, Ready set down his bread and took his own tin disk from his pocket. "Even when I'm the biggest toad in the puddle, Max, I'll always play buzzers with you."

In Philadelphia, buzzers had been a tame pastime played with strings and horn buttons. San Francisco newsboys played a much rougher version, using the tops of tin cans, which they sharpened around the edges. Bystanders had to duck quickly to avoid the loser's buzzer, which could fly off in unexpected directions when the string broke.

Ready won twice, which didn't seem to bother Max. "Want to come with us to the racetrack tomorrow? Who knows when you'll get another chance?"

"Tomorrow?" Ready asked. "The mail steamer's due."

Max laughed. "Well, if it comes in, we won't go. But if there's no sign of it, meet us at the omnibus at one o'clock."

As usual, Max would much rather spend money than earn it. Max's family needed the income as much as Ready's did. But that never stopped Max from spending his cash freely. But, why go to the races with a mail steamer due? That's when newsboys made some of their biggest profits.

"No, thanks." Ready tucked the bread under his arm. He needed every cent he could get his hands on before next Friday. Turning the corner towards home, he fervently hoped Charles wouldn't follow Max's bad example.

As Ready passed by the back entrance to the post office, a woman in a blue dress and hat stumbled out and almost crashed into him. Then she staggered into the street. Ready heard a thundering clatter and a shout from down the block.

"Runaway horse!"

The lady in blue was right in the horse's path. Ready raced into the street and shoved her out of the way, just as a horse and wagon careened past them. She fell in the gutter, he landed on top of her, and the bread went flying. When Ready tried to stand up, he slipped in the mud and banged his elbow against the edge of the wooden sidewalk. The woman scrambled to her feet.

A man in a long apron rushed out of a nearby store. "Are you injured?"

"I'm not." Ready rubbed his sore elbow. "How about you, ma'am?"

Re-pinning her hat, she gave a muffled reply. "No."

The shopkeeper shook his fist after the horse and wagon. Then he went back inside his store.

Ready tossed the ruined bread onto a nearby rubbish heap and turned back to the woman. To his surprise, it was the tall girl from the *Independence*. She seemed much older now, cleaned up and wearing nice clothes.

"My goodness," she said. "You're the little fellow who gave me the orange yesterday. And now you've helped me again. I am indebted to you."

Ignoring her "little fellow" comment, Ready tipped his cap. "Joseph Gates, at your service."

At that, the girl burst into tears again. "My brother's name is Joseph, and I don't know what's become of him!"

The girl looked younger again with tears streaming down her face. Ready wished he had a handkerchief to offer her.

"Excuse me, miss. Do you see that sign down the street that says Winn's? I have to go back there to buy bread. They happen to serve the finest dish of ice cream in San Francisco. May I buy you one?"

She brushed aside her tears and eyed him uncertainly.

"It's a perfectly respectable institution," Ready said. "They don't serve intoxicating liquors. Not even beer. Why Reverend Taylor himself would find nothing to preach against."

They walked to Winn's and ordered two dishes of ice cream. Ready hadn't splurged like this since he and Father had started saving for Mariposa. But it seemed the least he could do for a survivor of a shipwreck. And who knew when he'd see ice cream again?

The girl gazed in awe at the marble tables, marble floors, and crystal chandelier.

"Doesn't this surpass any ice cream saloon you've ever seen?" Ready asked proudly. Then he added, "I've told you my name. What's yours?"

"Lydia." Ready could barely hear her soft words. "Lydia Peckham." She tasted her ice cream. "It's like a strange dream. I'm in a palace, with a young redheaded boy I've just met. If only Joseph were here!"

Tears welled up in her eyes again. "The one thing that gave me strength during the horrible experience with the ship was my absolute certainty Joseph would be waiting for me in San Francisco. When he wasn't at the dock yesterday, I felt sure he'd find me at the hotel. I slept for fifteen hours, but there were no messages when I awoke."

She sighed heavily. "The ladies from the relief committee helped me clean up and gave me these clothes. When I hadn't heard from Joseph by noon, I went to the post office, to see if he'd left me a message. That's when I discovered that my last *four* letters to him—all written before I sailed from New York—have been sitting unclaimed for months. *He doesn't even know I've left New England.* I have no money. I have nowhere to go. And I don't know what to do!" She started crying again.

Ready leaned over. "I'll help you, Lydia. You don't have to be all alone!"

She dabbed at her eyes. "You are a sweet and brave boy, Joseph. You saved me from the horse, you bought me ice cream, and you're listening to me like a true friend. Thank you. But you can't be more than ten or eleven years old. Shouldn't you be in school? How could you help me?"

His reddened face almost matched his hair. "*Miss Peckham,*" Ready said gruffly. "I'm short and you're tall. But I'm not much younger than you. I'll be fifteen soon. I earn enough to pay my expenses, help with my family, and send money back east to my grandmother. I've been in San Francisco half a year and know it like the back of my hand. Next week, I'm leaving for the Mother Lode to make my pile. But I'm here now. Perhaps I can help you."

Lydia's pale cheeks flushed. "I'm sorry," she whispered.

Ready's tone softened. "Why did you come to San Francisco?"

23

Lydia's story unfolded as she ate her ice cream. She was sixteen, her brother Joseph twenty-one. Orphaned young, they'd been raised by an aunt in Vermont. A year earlier, Joseph had come west with several young men from their hometown. She'd received many glowing letters from him. He hadn't struck it rich, but usually found work wherever he went. He'd even found some gold. He urged her to come west, too.

"Aunt Clarissa took ill and died before Thanksgiving," Lydia said. "I wrote Joseph immediately and told him I'd leave for California after the New Year. I sent letters on different mail steamers, to make sure at least one reached him."

"How did you address them?"

"Mr. Joseph Peckham, in care of the San Francisco Post Office. He always received my letters before, even when he was up in the mountains."

In January, she'd left New York aboard the *Northern Light*, traveling with Miss Emily, an older lady known to her cousin in Vermont. They had reached Nicaragua in eleven days.

"It poured rain almost the entire time we crossed Nicaragua, and many passengers were sick," Lydia continued. "When we finally reached San Juan del Sud a week later and boarded the *Independence*, I thought things could only improve."

Her tears reappeared. "The wreck was ghastly," she whispered. "There weren't enough lifeboats, and then the ship caught fire. So many people died ...."

Lydia gazed blankly into the distance. After a moment, she spoke again. "Miss Emily made it to the island in one of the boats. I had to swim for it." She laughed ruefully. "My skirts ballooned up with air and helped keep me afloat! But the water was chilling cold, and I kept getting pushed back and forth by the waves."

"What did you do?"

"Just when I thought I would sink from exhaustion, a big wooden beam floated by. I grabbed for it, and so did a man floundering near me in the water. Together, we floated and kicked our way to shore."

"Then what?"

"The whole miserable lot of us—including the captain and most of the crew—huddled on that deserted island for three days. Our only food came from the carcasses of cattle that floated ashore from the wreckage. We had nothing to drink, until a barrel of molasses and a barrel of vinegar washed up. We mixed them together." She wrinkled her nose in disgust.

"Finally, a whaling ship saw our signal. Our captain hired the *Meteor* to bring us to San Francisco. The sailors on board were kind—one gave me his shoes—but the ship was crowded and smelly. I was seasick the whole time."

"And Miss Emily?"

"She did surprisingly well. She's strong. She leaves tomorrow for Marysville, where she and her brother keep a store. I could go with her, but I don't want to. I must find Joseph." She heaved another sigh. "I need to find work and a place to stay."

"Do you know how to sew?"

"Of course I know how to sew. What kind of question is that?"

Ready's eyes twinkled. "I think I can find you a job."

25

CHAPTER FOUR

The distant cannon blast of a ship entering San Francisco Bay woke Ready early Sunday. Taking care not to disturb his brothers, he crept out of bed and opened a window. Good, no fog to block the view. He climbed out and scrambled up a makeshift ladder to the roof. The sun was just peeking over the hills of Contra Costa to the east. Squinting at the signal tower atop Telegraph Hill, Ready saw the black wooden arms outstretched in the position that meant "side-wheel steamer." A white flag with the letters "U.S.M." fluttered above them. It was the mail ship, all right. Ducking back into the bedroom, he dressed and left before anyone else in the house had even stirred.

As Ready hurried towards Pacific Wharf, he marveled at how everything was falling into place. He and Father would leave San Francisco in five days. *Five days.* Within a week, he'd be standing in Agua Fria Creek, with a gold pan. And in few months, why, who knew how different life might be in a few months?

Even Mother was finally getting excited. When Marcus Seldon had first approached Father about Agua Fria Creek—about two months after they'd reached San Francisco—Mother had been dead set against it.

"You make more money at the factory than you ever did at home," she'd told her husband. "We came here together. We should stay together."

But Father had been adamant. "Vini, I didn't drag my family half-way around the world to make bricks. We came to California to get rich."

"San Francisco is a good place to earn money," Mother had insisted.

"And an even better place to *spend* it," Father had answered.

Ready agreed with Father. It had been smart to stay in San Francisco for the winter. But it was hideously expensive. It took four boarders, Father's job, and Ready's newspapers, just to get by. At this rate, the family would never get ahead.

Gradually, Mother had come around to Father's point of view. Yes, it would be lonely and hard to carry on in San Francisco without her husband and eldest son. But wasn't that a small price to pay for the chance to be wealthy? So, while Ready and his father had spent hours poring over books and magazine articles about gold mining, Mother had made her own preparations. She had started taking in sewing. Small jobs at first. Then bigger ones, like the order for the Congregational Church. But the large orders were proving to be too much work for Mother alone. That's why meeting Lydia had been such a stroke of good luck.

Ready's mother had hired Lydia immediately. Then she'd arranged for the girl to stay at Mrs. Salem's boarding house for ladies, a few doors away. Lydia would work part-time with Mother for pay, and part-time for Mrs. Salem for room and board.

By the time Ready reached Pacific Wharf, a huge crowd had gathered to greet the *John L. Stephens*. But while everyone else watched the approaching steamer, Ready kept his eye on a small boat belonging to the Adams Express Company. It rowed out to the large vessel, waited until someone heaved several bundles from the *John L. Stephens* and headed back.

When the rowboat reached the dock, the man on board flung one of the bundles into Ready's outstretched arms. The boy cut the string with his pocketknife and unwrapped a stack of newspapers. Tucking them under his arm, he pushed through the crowd. "*New York Herald*. Latest news from the east!"

"Right here, young man."

"Here, laddie, two for me."

"Over here, Red."

Ready's newspapers carried a date of March 5. They had left New York by ship exactly twenty-nine days before. They'd been unloaded at Panama, transported across the Isthmus, put on the *John L. Stephens*, and brought to San Francisco. What Ready held in his hands at that moment was the most current news from the eastern states available anywhere in town.

Tomorrow, the *Alta California* and other papers would reprint everything of interest, which anyone could buy for ten cents. Yet, so hungry were San Franciscans for news from home, Ready could easily sell these papers for fifty cents or a dollar, as long as he moved quickly.

Ready worked his way from the wharf to the center of town. Although it would take hours to sort the mail, a long line had already formed outside the post office.

"*New York Herald,* fresh off the steamer!"

"Over here, young'un." A heavyset fellow in a red flannel shirt held out two silver coins. "I'm from New York, and I haven't heard a word from home in over six months." The man snatched a paper and held the small print up close to his eyes. "President Pierce's inaugural address?" He scowled. "I was hoping for something more lively."

Ready laughed. "I don't write it, sir. Why don't you try page two?"

Inside, the post office lobby was noisy, hot, and stank of cigar smoke. Hundreds of men waited in line. Some sat on stools brought from home, though most stood, tapping their feet and shifting their weight in boredom.

"*New York Herald.*"

"Hey, you. Little red-haired feller!" a man shouted to Ready. "You think you've got the news with that there paper in your hand? I'll tell you some news. Forget about gold. I found me a soap mine at Table Mountain."

Ready knew a set-up for a tall tale when he heard one. He arched an eyebrow at the man. "A *soap* mine?"

"Yes, sir. The whole inside of Table Mountain is *clear soap.* A man just bores a square auger hole right into the side of the mountain until he gets into the soap. The pressure at the top causes it to be forced out, in a square bar. The man just has to clip it off at the right length, pack it, and ship it to market. That's a fact."

Ready laughed out loud. "I have irrefutable evidence you are not a teller of truth, my friend. Irrefutable evidence."

The man put on a look of mock anger. "And what evidence is that, young'un?"

"Anyone can see you haven't been *near* a bar of soap since you left the States!"

The huddled group broke into guffaws, the fellow himself laughing the loudest. He handed Ready a five-dollar gold piece, took a paper, and proceeded to entertain his companions with another story.

Ready sold his last paper at noon and stopped by the Adams Express office to settle accounts. There were no more *New York Heralds*, but he bought the last of the *Boston Journals* and ran home. He didn't want to miss what would be his last chance for Sunday dinner in quite a while.

His mother had already started ladling food at one end of the long kitchen table. Father sat at the other end. On one side sat the four boarders: Mr. and Mrs. Samuel Varnum, a couple in their forties from Pennsylvania, who had arrived on the *S.S. Lewis* with the Gates family; twenty-one-year-old Edward Baker, recently arrived from Connecticut; and twenty-two-year-old Harold Fitz, who'd come from New York the previous year. The men all worked with Ready's father at the brick factory. Mrs. Varnum decorated ladies' hats at a millinery shop. Harold Fitz also served as a volunteer fireman with the Monumental Engine Company.

On the other side of the table, Lydia, their invited guest, sat between Hugh and Charles. Ready removed his cap and quietly took his seat. The group was deep in discussion about what might have happened to Lydia's brother.

"If he was up in the mines, there is no doubt he was snowed in this past winter," Mr. Varnum told Lydia. "Roads and trails were closed for months. No one could get in or out, not even the express company stagecoaches."

"But the roads opened weeks ago," said Mrs. Varnum. "Surely, he would have sent for his mail."

"Melting snow has made for lots of flooding upriver," Ed Baker observed. "Some of the roads have closed again."

"Maybe he left California," Horace Fitz said. "Might have gone to Oregon. Or even Australia."

"Maybe he's sick," said Charles.

"Maybe he was *shanghaied*," little Hugh piped up.

Mrs. Gates glared at her youngest son. "Our guest has troubles enough. Don't heap on more with your imagination. Lydia, are you comfortable at Mrs. Salem's?"

"Yes, ma'am. Thank you for finding me such a pleasant place to stay."

"Mrs. Salem will have plenty to keep you busy. She doesn't have three strong boys to do chores at her house."

Charles shot a sour look at Ready. "*Two* strong boys do most of the work around here. And next week, it will only get worse."

"That's because one of the three is *really* a man, Charles," Ready answered. "Earning *real* money out in the world. This morning I sold fifty *New York Heralds*—and made twenty-nine dollars."

Ready's mother frowned. She considered public discussion of money to be very poor manners.

Then Lydia spoke up. "Joseph, I'm shocked you sell papers on the Sabbath!"

Ready snorted. "I sell papers when people want to buy them."

Mrs. Gates sighed. "Lydia, the Sabbath is practically ignored in San Francisco. Some people attend church. But there is hardly a break in business. People shop, go to the theater—not to mention the gambling houses and saloons. It's like any other day."

"Now, Mother," Mr. Gates said. "The girl will think she's dining with heathens. Lydia, we observe the day of rest as much as possible. In fact, this evening we'll read aloud from Mr. Dickens if you'd care to join us."

Dickens? Wouldn't Father's time be better spent reading about gold mining? "Not me," Ready said. "I'm catching the four o'clock steamer to Sacramento."

Mrs. Gates stiffened. Ready knew his mother didn't really approve of the newsboys traveling to Sacramento. Too many bad things might happen. But people upriver were starved for news, too, and the eastern papers always fetched a good price. His mother averted her eyes and said nothing.

CHAPTER FIVE

Ready arrived at the wharf with his newspapers hidden under his shirt and jacket. As he joined the passengers streaming up the gangway of the *Wilson G. Hunt,* he spotted Max and two other newsboys ahead of him. *Dad-blame it.* Why had he dawdled? Now, the others would get the best hiding spots.

At the top of the gangway, most passengers turned right. But Ready went left, climbed down a ladder, and ducked into the cargo storage room. He heard a sharp hiss.

"*Pssssssssss.* Get out!"

It was Max, crouched between two crates. "*Vamoose.* There's only room for one here—me!"

Ready stuck out his tongue at Max. If he left the cargo room now, he'd get caught. Rather than turn back, Ready squeezed between the crates to a door on the opposite wall. It led to another storage chamber. He peered into it. No room to hide here, either. Another door on the far side stood slightly ajar. He crept down the crowded aisle and peeked through. The engine room. Though the machinery hummed, no one was there.

Just then, Ready heard voices. People were coming! He slipped into the engine room and closed the door behind him. But before he could figure out his next move, he saw a man's boot descending from a ladder on the far wall. He dove into a small space behind an iron post. Huddled in this cubbyhole, he breathed a sigh of relief.

Once the engine got underway, however, Ready realized he'd chosen a terrible hiding place. The tight spot didn't even give him room to shift his weight. His legs were cramped, sweat rolled down his face, and the stench of hot grease made him sick to his stomach. But worst of all, every few seconds a heavy piece of iron machinery slammed down in front of him, only inches from his body. His heart pounded as he struggled to keep panic from overtaking him. He had to get out of there immediately!

"HELLO!"

The man obviously couldn't hear him.

"HELLLLLOOOO."

No good. Ready simply could not shout louder than the roaring engine. What could he do? Bracing himself for the next deafening slam of the iron arm, he imagined Max standing at Montgomery and Clay, calling, "EXTRA. Extra! Newsboy crushed in river boat accident!" *No thanks. I'll get my name in the paper some day when I can read it myself.*

He counted the interval between slams. *One, two, three, four.* Was that enough time to hurl himself out of harm's way before the iron arm returned? *One, two, three, four.* He thought he could do it. But if he failed, he'd be pulverized! *One, two, three, four.*

He pictured his mother reading her Bible. The only prayer he could think of was, "Deliver us from evil." That iron arm looked mighty evil. *One, two, three, four.*

Ready took a deep breath, counted for the right moment, and lunged. He felt himself scream, but the sound was swallowed up by the din of the engine. He crashed against a wall and lay panting on the floor, relieved he was still in one piece. At any moment, he expected the engine man to grab him by the scruff of the neck and haul him to the captain.

But to Ready's astonishment, the man never knew he was there. Gingerly moving his sore legs, Ready crept back through the door to the cargo hold.

Max popped out from between the crates. "I'm sure they've collected the tickets by now. Shall we go back up?"

When the *Wilson G. Hunt* reached Sacramento at two a.m., the river was higher than Ready had ever seen it. And unlike the carnival atmosphere that usually greeted San Francisco steamers, even in the middle of the night, things were quiet. Once he left the boat, Ready saw why.

More than a foot of muddy water covered Front Street. No crowd of spectators eager for month-old news from the States waited there. No fast-talking hotel runners bellowed: *Fine accommodations! Best prices!* No line of wagons stood ready for passengers and luggage. Only a few lights shone from windows on Front Street.

"The levee broke three hours ago," a steamship agent told the passengers. "Most of the city is flooded. If you're continuing upriver on the next boat, you can leave your luggage here. There's an upstairs saloon open on Front Street. Some of you may want to wait there."

Ready gazed glumly at the dark water. He had hoped to earn at least twenty more dollars on this trip. Instead, he'd almost gotten himself killed, he was out the money for the *Boston Journals*, and would likely ruin his only shoes wading to the saloon. Well, he couldn't stand on the dock for ten hours. Max and the others had already plunged into the flooded street. Reluctantly, Ready followed.

Wet and muddy passengers soon filled the saloon. Ready warmed himself with hot coffee and took the *Boston Journals* out of his shirt.

"You could dry your shoes with those," Max said. "You won't find any other use for them. Come on, let's try our luck with the cards."

Dry shoes with his precious newspapers? Not likely. Ready watched Max walk over to the faro table. *Max came in here with his pockets full of money, and he'll walk out as poor as Job's turkey*, Ready thought. *What a lunkhead!*

Unlike his grandmother, Ready didn't think gambling was a sin. He just thought it a foolish waste of hard-earned cash. Max had one of the best jobs a boy could have in San Francisco, but he threw his money away before it ever got a chance to get acquainted with his pocket. Ready shook his head with exasperation.

Now, who might buy his newspapers? Nobody from the *Wilson G. Hunt*. They'd had their chance in San Francisco. Who else? He took the papers to the saloonkeeper. "These *Boston Journals* are fresh off the eastern steamer. You could sell them to your customers later today."

The proprietor shook his head. "I won't have any more customers 'til the levee is fixed. Might take a few days. By then, all that news in your hand will have been published in the *Sacramento Union*."

Then he pointed across the room. "See that man over there? He's a traveling daguerreotypist. He pulls a wagonload of equipment all through the mining region, charging two dollars for a likeness. He passes through some remote areas. Maybe he'd buy your papers."

The saloonkeeper led Ready over to the man. "Clarence, this boy has a stack of the latest *Boston Journals*. You could sell them to those homesick miners who come to you for portraits."

The daguerreotypist rose politely. Ready was startled to find he could look him right in the eye without tipping back his head. This full-grown man, with a suit, beard, and waxed mustache, was barely taller than Ready himself.

"Clarence Wallace," the man said, shaking Ready's hand. "Perhaps we can work something out."

Ready sat in the offered chair. "Your traveling portrait gallery must not fare too well on these flooded streets, sir."

Mr. Wallace smiled. "My wagon is stored in a barn near Marysville. I took the steamer to San Francisco for supplies."

Temporarily forgetting about his *Boston Journals*, Ready peppered the dageurreotypist with questions. How long did it take to learn his craft? Where did he get his camera and chemicals? Had he ever made a portrait of a famous person?

Mr. Wallace happily talked about his work. He'd come to California two years earlier, bringing camera and supplies with him. When his own attempts to find gold had faltered, he'd outfitted a wagon as a moving studio. Most of his customers were argonauts—gold seekers—wanting to send likenesses to the folks back home.

"Back east, when people have a portrait made, they dress up in their Sunday best." The daguerreotypist chuckled. "California is different. Men want to look like gold miners, even if they haven't found a speck of dust. They'll wear their roughest clothes and hold pickaxes in their hands."

Sometimes, people wanted pictures of their house or their farm or even their horse. He'd made images of dead people before burial, Indians in native dress, and several poses of the famous pioneer John Sutter. Mr. Wallace brought out a small leather case. Inside was a likeness of the daguerreotypist himself, standing in front of a strange-looking wagon. It looked like a little house on wheels, with windows, a door, and *Wallace's Daguerrian Saloon* painted on the side.

"I'm teaching my new assistant how to use the equipment," Mr. Wallace explained. "He made that last week." Mr. Wallace returned the case to his pocket. "I'm eager to get back to work. This past winter's nasty weather put me out of business for several months. Roads were impassible, and all my supplies froze." The daguerreotypist tapped a fingernail on Ready's *Boston Journals*. "I don't have much cash left after new supplies. But I can give you something for your papers."

They settled on enough to cover a meal at the saloon and a return ticket to San Francisco. Ready would travel as an official paying customer on the trip back.

CHAPTER SIX

On board the steamer heading back to San Francisco, passengers were abuzz over news of the latest "color" found on the banks of the Feather River.

"I hear there's gold in every gulch and ravine," one man explained to Ready. "All that melting snow loosens the gold and washes it downstream."

"I don't understand, sir."

"What don't you understand, son?"

"Why are you heading to San Francisco instead of to the Feather River?"

The man chuckled. "I'm wondering that myself."

Ready drifted to a corner and pondered this information. Should he and Father head for the Feather River instead? They didn't want to waste their time searching in the wrong spot. But, no. Heavy snow had fallen throughout the gold region. All the rivers were running high. That would include Agua Fria Ceek, where Marcus Seldon had a cabin waiting for them. Everything should work out just fine. It was Monday afternoon. Four days to go.

When the steamer docked in San Francisco, Ready raced home. To his surprise, it was Lydia who met him at the door, with a worried look on her face.

"What happened?" Ready asked in alarm. "Where *is* everybody?"

"I'm so sorry," Lydia said. "Your father is at the city hospital. A load of bricks fell on him."

Ready's mother seemed strangely calm when he found her at the hospital. He sat, stunned, as she explained that Father's broken leg and broken arm would keep him laid up for months. The trip to Agua Fria Creek was, of course, now completely out of the question. The whole family would stay in San Francisco.

His mother spoke briskly. "We'll get extra beds and squeeze in more boarders. I'll take in more sewing. You'll keep selling newspapers. Your brothers will find jobs. We'll manage. Getting Father well is our most important task now."

"Of course, Mother." Ready tried to sound more stalwart than he felt. He kept his emotions bottled up on the walk home. But when he crept into bed beside his slumbering brothers, Ready's true feelings came tumbling out. He lay in bed sobbing—for Father, for the family, for himself. For lost opportunities. For that big nugget just waiting to be found on the banks of Agua Fria Creek.

The following days passed in a blur. The boys moved their bed to an alcove on the first floor, separated from the kitchen by a curtain. Their former room now housed three new boarders—young men recently arrived from Connecticut.

Though Ready continued to hawk the *Alta California*, business was slow. Without much going on, few people bought papers. In the afternoons, he did what was needed at home. He measured and cut green velvet. He hauled water and firewood. He swept the house, buried garbage in the back yard, and dragged rugs outside for a thorough beating. Almost hourly, he climbed on the roof to check the signal tower, watching for the next side-wheel steamer with eastern newspapers. He tried not to think about Agua Fria Creek.

But in bed at night, it was all he could think about. He envisioned himself scooping up handfuls of sand sparkling with golden flecks. He imagined digging through rocks on the river bank with his crevicing spoon. Sometimes, he pictured himself walking into an assay office with a hunk of gold and having the man behind the counter exclaim, "It's the biggest nugget I've ever seen!" Then, he'd remember the sight of Father's bruised and broken body, and plunge into despair again.

One day, he overheard Lydia tell his mother she'd written to her cousins in Vermont. "I explained about the *Independence* and about Joseph," she said. "Maybe there are letters from him back home even now, explaining where he is."

Eager for a break, Ready set down the wood he'd been stacking in the kitchen. "It's Steamer Day, Lydia," he called into the parlor. "Shall I take the letter to the post office for you?"

Ready's mother surveyed the finished cushions in the corner of the room. "Lydia, you've worked hard all day. You deserve some fresh air. Why don't you both go?"

Although the post office was crowded, the line at the ladies' window was short. After posting Lydia's letter, the clerk checked on Joseph Peckham's mail again. Still there, and no messages for Lydia.

Her shoulders sagged. Then, she pulled a crumpled piece of paper from her handbag, turned to Ready and said, "Where is Dupont Street?"

"Not far."

He took the paper from her hand, an advertisement torn from the *Alta California*, and read aloud: "*Madame de Cassins, the celebrated Diviner, explains the Past and predicts the future. Can be consulted in English, French, Italian, Greek, Arabic and Russian from 9-5, and 7-10 PM, No. 304 Dupont St., between Broadway and Vallejo.*"

His eyebrows shot up. "A fortune-teller?"

Lydia's words came out in an excited jumble. "One of the ladies at Mrs. Salem's told me Madame de Cassins is the genuine article. She consulted her when she first arrived, and Madame knew which ship she'd come on and where she was from. She even told her she'd find work right away—and she did."

Ready harrumphed. "Madame de Cassins probably reads the shipping news in the *Alta California*. And anybody can work in San Francisco. Look at you. You started two days after the *Meteor* dumped you on the wharf."

"Madame helped someone else locate a lost ring."

Ready wrinkled his nose with scorn. "Lydia, you can't *believe* that hocus-pocus!"

Lydia bit her lip. Then, she whispered, "Maybe she can help me find my brother."

Ready regretted his harsh manner. Maybe going to this quack would make Lydia feel better. He softened his tone. "I know Dupont Street, Lydia. I'll take you there."

The outside of Madame de Cassins' white clapboard house looked like the Gates' home, except for a small sign that read "Diviner—initial consultation $2." But the inside was vastly different. A Chinese servant dressed in green silk ushered them into a room filled with curious objects—carved teak chairs, brass lamps that might have held Aladdin's genie, a chest decorated with strange symbols.

Ready pointed to the chest. "Probably keeps her magic potions in that one."

"Shhhh," Lydia hissed. "She might hear you."

"If she can read our minds, she knows what I'm thinking anyway."

At that moment, a plump woman with dark cascading hair swept into the room. Layers of gold chains jangled at her neck and wrists. Brightly colored clothing swirled about her. She grasped Lydia's hand. "You have had a long and difficult journey, my child," she said in heavily accented English. "You have a troubled heart."

Lydia pressed some coins into the gypsy's hands, as tears welled up in her eyes. "It's my brother. I fear something terrible has happened to him."

Madame de Cassins led Lydia to a red brocade sofa. "Sit. Tell me."

As Lydia poured out her story, Ready studied his fingernails. What was the fortune-teller up to? The sign said the *initial* consultation was $2. Two bucks per customer wouldn't pay the rent on this place. The gypsy probably used the first visit to set her hooks, to keep the person coming back for more. How many poor fools traipsed in here with their tales of woe, and how much cash did Madame de Cassins wring out of them?

After Lydia finished her story, Madame sat with her eyes closed and her fingers pressed against her forehead. Then she opened her eyes and spoke. "All is well. You and your brother will find each other. Be patient and strong." The gypsy stood up.

"That's IT?" Ready leapt to his feet. "For two dollars, all you can say is *be patient?* Lydia, get your money back!"

Madame de Cassins smiled. "Children often don't understand the value of patience. With years, you will."

Ready's face flushed. "If you polished up your crystal ball, you'd see I'm *not* a child. I understand perfectly well about charlatans who prey on people in dire circumstances."

The gypsy nodded. "You are quick to fight, you with the red hair. That may help you in life. But you are mistaken if you think this girl is in dire circumstances."

"But I *am*," Lydia protested. "I don't know what to do."

"Nonsense. You are strong and intelligent. California offers opportunities. You will make the most of them."

Madame led them to the door. "Your heart is troubled, too," she told Ready. "Your worry is not so different from hers—finding your place in an uncertain world." She paused. "You also wish you were taller."

Ready blushed more, and Lydia hid a smile behind her hand. They walked out of the house and down the stairs to the sidewalk, before they both burst out laughing. They laughed all the way to the corner and across the street.

"You've had a long and difficult journey, my child," Ready intoned, imitating the gypsy's accent. "As if anyone could come to San Francisco without a long and difficult journey!"

"I feel ridiculous, Joseph." Lydia sighed. "Back in Vermont I would never have gone to a fortune-teller. What could I have been thinking?"

"People do lots of things in San Francisco they wouldn't do back home, Lydia. Why, next thing, you'll be dealing cards at the El Dorado and smoking cigars."

After a moment, Lydia asked, "Why do people call you Ready?"

"My father started calling me that when I was three or four. Partly for my hair, of course. But, mostly because he said I was always ready to do anything, whether it was a good idea or not." He gave a small smile. "I suppose that's still true."

Lydia gazed far into the distance. "When I was little, I called my brother 'Joey Bub.' And he called me 'Sissy Lid.' We still use those names in private from time to time." She exhaled loudly. "Or rather, we used to."

"Lydia." Ready stopped walking. "I don't think Madame de Cassins has any special powers. But, she's right about one thing. You will find your brother, I'm sure of it."

A tear ran down Lydia's cheek. "What if he's dead?"

"Don't even talk like that. He's alive and we'll find him. You and I will find him."

"How?"

"I haven't figured that part out yet. But I'm working on it."

CHAPTER SEVEN

Ready waited in vain to sell eastern newspapers that week. The ship that would have brought them, the *S.S. Lewis,* ran aground in heavy fog just north of the Golden Gate. Luckily, everyone on board made it safely ashore before the ship split apart and sank. Rescue boats retrieved the passengers and brought them to San Francisco.

The *S.S. Lewis* had held a special place in Ready's heart, ever since it had brought the Gates family to California. He remembered climbing the ship's rigging as they entered the harbor, and how San Francisco had sparkled in the morning sun. Back then, Ready had assumed he'd find a king's ransom of gold before his fifteenth birthday. Now, the *S.S. Lewis*—and his dreams—had both been smashed on the rocks of fate.

Father was home from the hospital now. It had taken three big men to get him out of the hired carriage and up the stairs to the bedroom. Ready didn't see him much. Both parents said Ready could help best by earning as much money as he possibly could.

Suddenly, Ready was plenty busy. The sinking of the *S.S. Lewis* was the first in a string of events that put the newsboys back to work full time. The steamboat *Jenny Lind* exploded near San Jose, killing twenty-one people. Heavy rains and winds struck San Francisco, flooding roads, destroying houses, and damaging ships in the harbor. And a hotly contested city election kept politicians flinging charges back and forth.

Each day after Ready sold his papers, he'd look for other work. Sometimes, a produce man hired him to run errands and paid him in fruit and vegetables. A shopkeeper had him carry packages and gave him stationery and ink. Once, Ready distributed handbills for a theater show and received a free ticket. He would have liked to see the play himself. But, he sold the ticket to Max and turned the money over to his mother.

He worked hard, but his heart wasn't in it. Ready didn't want to run errands in San Francisco—he wanted to find gold! Sometimes, he daydreamed about striking out on his own. How hard could it be?

Helping Lydia look for her brother became a welcome distraction for Ready. Together, they placed an ad in the *Alta California*, seeking information about the whereabouts of Joseph Peckham. And whenever Ready passed the post office, he'd stop to see if anyone had picked up Joseph's mail. Before long, the clerks knew him by name.

One Sunday, Lydia asked Ready to take her to see Reverend William Taylor. "Mrs. Salem says he's been preaching in these streets since '49, and he knows things nobody else knows. I want to ask him about *shanghaiing*."

Ready took Lydia to the plaza, where a huge crowd thronged about a man standing on a barrel singing, "ALL PRAISES TO OUR GOD AND KING...."

They climbed on top of a wooden crate to see better. Reverend Taylor finished his hymn and began to preach in thundering tones.

"I have for my pulpit today *a barrel of whisky*. Probably the first time this barrel has ever been put to good use!"

A chuckle rippled through the crowd.

"The 'critter' in this barrel will do me no harm while I keep it under my feet. And I say to you all, keep the critter *under your feet*, and you will have nothing to fear from it."

The minister spotted Ready standing on the crate and pointed at him. "After a shipwreck, San Francisco newsboys cry out the tidings, and people mourn and fret over every detail. But *souls*, precious *souls*, are wrecked in our midst daily—wrecked on the shoals of whisky and gambling. As these souls drift down the gulf stream of despair into the maelstrom of hell, *nothing* is said about it, *no* paper announces the disaster, *nobody* mourns the loss. But I tell you, even *one* human soul is worth more than all the ships in the world!"

After the sermon, Ready explained Lydia's plight to Reverend Taylor.

"Is there a way to know if my brother has been shanghaied?" she asked.

Reverend Taylor fingered his mutton chop whiskers. "The system of shanghaiing is an ancient one," he began slowly, "though the term is a California invention. After the discovery of gold, hundreds of ships began to arrive in San Francisco harbor every day. But when it came time to leave, the captains often found their crew had jumped ship to look for gold. So, captains needed to find sailors for their return voyages.

"Thus began a despicable practice of drugging men with a compound of whisky, brandy, gin, and opium, which put them into a long sleep. When the poor fellows woke up, they found themselves on a ship headed for Shanghai, or some other distant destination, and nothing to be done about it."

"That's *monstrous*." Lydia's eyes grew wide. "This still goes on?"

"Despite efforts to stop it, the practice continues. Too many people get rich from it. But regarding your brother, my dear. Did he imbibe in strong drink?"

Lydia shook her head. "We came from a temperance family. Even in his letters, Joseph spoke of strictly avoiding all spirits and gambling."

The minister nodded thoughtfully. "Most of the sharks who carry out this scheme find their victims in saloons and gaming houses. Where was your brother when you last heard from him?"

"San Francisco."

"Did he ever work as a sailor or spend time with sailors?"

She shook her head again. "He was seasick on the entire voyage west. He had no desire to be a sailor."

"The sharks tend to work where sailors congregate. Of course, if they're desperate, they'll take anyone they can find."

The preacher stood up. "Your brother probably went looking for gold. This past winter was a hard one. There's a lot of unclaimed mail at the post office. Come summer, he may very well turn up."

Reverend Taylor held up his leather-bound Bible. "Do you have a copy of God's Holy Word, my dear?"

"My Bible sank with the *Independence*, Reverend. But the relief committee gave me a new one."

"Read it daily and trust in the Lord." The minister nodded towards Ready. "And why not read some to our red-headed friend here? He's a good boy, but San Francisco leads many a virtuous person away from the straight and narrow path."

CHAPTER EIGHT

Later that night, as Ready crept into bed, he found Charles peering at him in the dim light. "Go to sleep," Ready whispered. "Don't wake up Hugh."

"I *can't* sleep," Charles whispered back. "I need to tell you something." He got out of bed and put his coat on over his nightshirt. "Let's go out on the back porch."

Mystified, Ready put on his own coat and followed his brother outside.

Charles hugged himself in the chilly night air. "I overheard Mother talking with Mrs. Varnum tonight. She's very upset."

"About what?"

"Everything. She's worried about Father. The landlord's going to raise our rent. And Cousin Margaret wrote that Grandma is sick again. She wants us to send more money for doctor bills and medicine."

Ready's heart sank. His days were already filled with work. How could he possibly earn any more money?

"Can you get me on at the *Alta*?" Charles asked. "I could quit school and sell papers. That's what I would have done anyway, if you and Father had gone to Mariposa."

Ready shook his head. "There aren't any openings."

"How about the produce man? I could run errands, too."

He shrugged. "Maybe. But he doesn't pay cash."

Ready leaned against the porch railing and gazed out into the moonlight. An idea had been percolating in his head for some time now. What if he were to travel to Mariposa by himself? He could stay with Marcus Seldon and help him work the creek bed. Charles could take over Ready's job at the newspaper and run errands for the fruit vendor, too.

He started to tell Charles his idea, but stopped himself. Ready needed to think about it more. Mother would hate it, he knew. Better to have the details worked out before raising the subject. But Charles needed some kind of assurance now.

As Ready glanced at the moonlit back yard, a discarded tin can caught his eye. He retrieved it and brought it back to Charles. "Have you ever noticed how many tin cans are thrown away on the rubbish heaps of San Francisco every day?"

Without waiting for an answer, Ready continued, "Hundreds, maybe thousands. Do you know what solder is?"

Charles shook his head. "Sodder?"

"See that line running down one side of this can? That's solder," Ready said. "It's a mixture of lead and tin that holds pieces of metal together. If you put a tin can in a fire that's hot enough, the solder will melt and run off. Like wax rolling down a candle. When it cools and hardens, it's called pig lead."

Charles giggled. "*Pig lead?* Why?"

"I don't know. But I've heard metalsmiths will buy it by the pound. After school tomorrow, have Hugh help you gather all the empty cans you can find. Let's experiment and see how much money we can make."

Charles looked doubtful. "I suppose it's worth a try."

One afternoon a few days later, Ready came across the Monumental Engine Company struggling to pull a heavy pumper up a steep hill. One of the firemen was Horace Fitz, who boarded at the Gates home. Ready watched in fascination as the men finally reached the top of the hill, reversed the ropes, and carefully lowered the engine back down the sharp incline.

At the end of the training drill, Ready spoke to Horace. "How much does that contraption weigh?"

"This iron tub on wheels?" Horace asked. "At least a thousand pounds."

Ready gave a low whistle. "How often do you pull it uphill like that?"

"We usually practice once a month. But we wanted some extra preparation before next week's dread date."

"Dread date?"

"May fourth is the anniversary of two of San Francisco's worst fires—in 1850 and '51. Some crazy person may try to mark the occasion by setting the town on fire again."

Now Ready remembered. He'd heard men at the *Alta* talking about it recently. The fire of '51 had laid waste to eighteen square blocks. Flames had raced along the wooden streets, destroying almost two thousand buildings. Desperate to stop the inferno, firemen had blown up some houses with dynamite. But the fire had leapt across the gaps and kept going. The glowing sky could be seen for a hundred miles.

Ready frowned. "Could that happen again?"

Horace shrugged. "We have better equipment, our alarm bell can now be heard all over town, and we've built water cisterns below the main streets. But we'd be foolish to let down our guard."

Each evening, Ready counted out his earnings for his mother. Then, he'd read Father the newspaper, picking out items that seemed most interesting. Like where the latest gold discoveries were, and how high the rivers were running. How it had taken six men to rescue a horse whose leg had slipped through a broken board on Long Wharf. That Lola Montez, the world-famous dancer, was coming to California. And that an aeronaut named Mr. Kelly was bringing a hot-air balloon to San Francisco.

Father's eyes lit up at mention of the balloon. "Remember back home, when we watched the great John Wise take up his balloon?"

"I remember how long we waited out there in the country," Ready said. "I remember how hot and thirsty I was."

Though he couldn't devote much time to it, Ready still wanted to help Lydia find her brother. But other than placing an advertisement, he didn't know what to do. He agreed with the preacher that Joseph was probably working a gold claim right now. But where to search for someone who could be anywhere?

Ready questioned Lydia closely about Joseph's past letters. Did she recall specific places he had mentioned? Anywhere he had worked? Anyone he had met? Nothing she remembered gave any clue to his possible whereabouts. Ready tried another angle. "Tell me again what he looks like."

"Tall, thin, brown hair."

"And how tall did you say he is?"

"Six-foot five."

Ready laughed in disbelief. "You omitted that detail before, Lydia! Your brother is six-foot *five*?"

"Our parents were both tall. I'm five-foot nine, you know."

"Is there anything else unusual about how he looks?"

Lydia nodded. "He broke his nose when he was ten. It healed badly—rather pushed over to one side. The other boys teased him unmercifully."

"So, we're looking for an exceedingly tall man with a crooked nose," Ready mused. "People would notice him in a crowd, don't you think? They might remember him later."

He knew it was a long shot. But, after that, if Ready encountered someone returning from the mining region, he'd ask about Joseph. However, no one remembered a very tall young man with a bent nose.

One day, Ready saw Reverend Taylor walking down the street with another man. The minister's companion turned out to be Brother Brewster, a preacher leaving the next day to start a new church in Placerville. Brother Brewster listened intently to Ready's story and promised to keep an eye out for Joseph Peckham.

"But I wouldn't get my hopes up, lad," he cautioned. "I've traveled the mining towns since '51. I can't tell you how many funerals I've performed. Men fall from horses, slip into raging streams, or catch the fever and die. The luckier ones have friends who notify their families back home. But others are known only as 'One-eyed Pete,' or 'Crazy Charlie.' When they're gone, they're gone, and no one's the wiser."

After leaving Brother Brewster, Ready once again stopped by the post office.

"Still here," the clerk said. "The Peckham letters are still here."

CHAPTER NINE

On May second, Ready sold papers in the morning and delivered boxes of produce in the afternoon. As he passed the post office, he realized he hadn't checked on Lydia's letters in two days.

No sooner had he crossed the threshold, than a clerk bellowed at him. "Ready Gates! Frank Wyman picked up letters for more than a hundred men this morning, including your Joseph Peckham."

He raced over to the counter. "Who's Wyman?"

"A private agent. Men pay to register their names, and Wyman picks up their mail. The hard winter put him out of business for a while. But he's back at it now."

"How can I find him?"

The clerk leaned across the counter with a conspiratorial whisper. "He's staying at the Rassette House."

Ready sprinted to the five-story hotel at the corner of Sansome and Bush, and inquired for Frank Wyman.

"Aye, Mr. Wyman is registered here," a clerk with a Scottish accent told him. "But he's out."

Ready left a note for the agent and then ran home. He found his mother in the kitchen. "Where's Lydia? I have news about her brother!"

"What?"

Ready briefly explained. "Do you think she's at Mrs. Salem's?"

His mother's tired face brightened. Was it her first smile since Father's accident? "Our Lydia has a social engagement tonight. She's been invited to dinner and the theater with a young man. A very *suitable* young man, I might add."

Ready snorted. "Suitable for *what?*"

His mother looked at him sharply. "Regardless of her brother, Lydia must start planning her own future. She's almost seventeen. She doesn't want to go back to Vermont. The sooner she finds herself a good husband, the better off she'll be."

"A *husband?*" Ready protested. "She's young. She doesn't have to worry about a husband yet."

"You sound just like Lydia when I suggested she accept Horace's invitation."

"Horace? You mean Horace Fitz, our boarder?" *The strong, good-looking fireman?*

His mother nodded. "He's a promising young man. He has a steady job, writes to his mother often, and attends church regularly. And I can tell he's been sweet on Lydia since the day they met."

Mrs. Gates brushed a speck from her sleeve. "He only needed a little encouragement to invite her out."

Ready stared at his mother. "Encouragement? *You* arranged this?"

His mother sighed. "I'm too busy to arrange *anyone's* social life, young man. But when Horace confided his interest in Lydia, I suggested he pursue it."

She smiled again. "You're not the only one who can help a damsel in distress, Ready. You find the brother, I'll find the husband."

"The *brother*." Ready slapped his forehead. He had forgotten about Frank Wyman! "Where are she and Horace going tonight?"

"To dine at a French restaurant and then see Mrs. Baker at the Adelphi Theater. She's gotten such wonderful reviews."

"Don't hold supper for me!"

Ready tried three French restaurants, without any luck. He'd have to catch Lydia and Horace at the theater. He arrived at the Adelphi just before curtain time. Should he wait around outside until it was over? After shivering in the wind for a few minutes, he bought the cheapest seat available and went inside. Besides, people always raved about what a great actress Mrs. Baker was. Now, Ready could see for himself.

The first play, *The Bride of Lammermoor,* was a tragedy based on a novel by Sir Walter Scott. But Ready couldn't concentrate on the performance. What if the hotel clerk didn't give Wyman the note? What if the agent changed his plans and left tonight? Maybe Ready shouldn't have tried to find Lydia. Maybe he should have stayed at the Rassette House until Wyman appeared. Well, at least the agent had Joseph's letters. When her brother received them, he'd know Lydia was waiting in San Francisco.

Ready continued to brood. When the curtain closed and the lights came on, he stood in the balcony searching the theater below for Lydia and Horace. Then he prowled the lobby. No sign of them. He went back to the balcony and finally spotted them returning to their seats. Then the lights went down. He'd have to sit through another performance.

The second play, also starring Mrs. Baker, was a comedy called *Married Life*. All this talk of brides and marriage! Had his mother chosen the theater bill, too? Though he would never admit it to a living soul, Ready felt stabs of jealousy. Lydia was the only girl who had ever paid any attention to him at all. They were good friends and partners in looking for her brother. Now, she was being swept off her feet by a handsome fireman. In frustration, Ready kicked at the seat in front of him. The man sitting there turned and scowled. Ready mumbled an apology.

Why was it that at sixteen, Lydia was considered a woman, old enough for courtship and marriage? When Ready himself turned sixteen, he'd still be considered a boy. And why this rush to marry off Lydia? He knew his mother worried about the girl. But marriage? A drastic step. Thank goodness Frank Wyman had shown up. He would lead them to Lydia's brother, and Ready's mother could get out of the matchmaking business.

After the final curtain, Ready found Lydia and Horace in the lobby. With grudging admiration, he noticed Horace's freshly barbered hair and new suit of clothes. Lydia must have gone shopping, too. She didn't get that green silk dress from the relief committee! He hated to admit they made an attractive couple.

Lydia was elated to hear about Frank Wyman. Eager to leave for the Rassette House, the three moved towards the theater's front door. But a commotion outside blocked their way. People in the street ran and shouted, horses neighed, and a bell clanged insistently in the distance.

When they finally made it outside, the air smelled of smoke and the sky glowed orange. A dozen brawny men raced down the street pulling a fire engine.

"It's the Monumentals," Horace exclaimed. "I must join them!" He tore off his coat and thrust it at Ready. "Take this, please, and see Lydia home." Then he disappeared into the chaotic night.

Ready called out to a bystander. "What's on fire?"

"That big hotel at Sansome and Bush!"

The Rassette House? He grabbed Lydia's hand and started running. Lydia hitched up her skirts and kept up with him, as they sidestepped horses, wagons, and people. When they passed by the fenced yard behind his friend Max's house, Ready flung Horace's coat and his own into the enclosure and kept running.

"I'll get them tomorrow," he puffed to Lydia.

At the corner of Sansome and Bush, they saw a wall of flames shooting out in all directions. Smoke bright with flying sparks billowed into the night sky. Ready could see that the Monumentals had dropped their suction hose into the cistern under Bush Street. Eight men feverishly worked the pumper rails, sucking water up into the tank and shooting it out the large brass nozzle on top. The intense heat vaporized the water before it even touched the flames. The men pumped on.

There were firemen everywhere, at least a hundred of them, carrying ladders and hoses and axes. Hotel guests in nightclothes huddled across the street, watching. But not everyone was out yet. Some waited on ledges for the firemen to reach them with ladders. Others simply jumped. Then, in the distance, beyond the firemen, Ready noticed a small figure dangling from the hotel's second-story ledge. Could it be a *child?*

He broke into a strong run, dodging firemen, hoses, and spraying water. He looked up to see a little girl surrounded by flames, a look of terror on her face. Just as her fingers lost their grip, Ready stretched out his arms to catch her. Her weight pushed him backwards. To his surprise, Lydia stood right behind him, breaking his fall. Together, the three ran for safety, the child sobbing against Ready's shoulder.

When Ready and Lydia returned to the corner of Sansome and Bush the next morning, all they found was a pile of black rubble. Not a plank of wood nor scrap of fabric had escaped the flames. In what had been the hotel kitchen, the charred remnants of a stove were covered with melted pots and pans. But though the fire had destroyed the Rassette House and eleven other buildings, the rest of the city was spared. Horace Fitz and his fellow firemen had done their job well.

To their relief, Ready and Lydia learned that no one had died. But it took them all day to locate Frank Wyman. He was at the city hospital, with burns, cuts, and a broken foot.

"I was asleep, when a loud noise woke me," the agent whispered. "Then I realized the floor, the walls, the door, everything around me, was on fire. I ran to the window, smashed the glass, and jumped through it."

He grimaced in pain. "Luckily, I was only on the second floor."

Lydia spoke gently. "Mr. Wyman. What about the letters?"

"Ashes."

Lydia persisted. "Do you remember Joseph Peckham? Where were you supposed to give him his letters?"

The agent shook his head feebly. "I registered men from Downieville to Placerville. My list burned up, too. I don't remember Joseph Peckham."

CHAPTER TEN

Ready kicked himself for days. Why hadn't he waited for Mr. Wyman in the hotel lobby? If he had spoken with the agent before the fire, Lydia might be reunited with her brother by now. Instead, they were farther from finding Joseph Peckham than when they'd started, and Lydia was gloomier than ever.

Things were no better with his own family. Father remained weak and miserable. Every day, Mother worked her fingers to the bone and fretted about Grandma back home. In addition, two of the new boarders had moved out. Now, the family had to spend precious money on newspaper ads to fill their places.

Each day, Ready sold papers, delivered produce, and helped out at home. But it wasn't enough. His family needed more money. It was as simple as that. And they weren't going to get it if they just kept doing the same things over and over.

They needed a new plan. Actually, Ready felt they needed to go back to their original plan—finding gold. Gold was why they'd come to California, and it was what would save them now. It seemed so obvious to him. Why couldn't his parents see it?

Then one day Father received a letter from Marcus Seldon, which Mother read aloud. Agua Fria Creek was running high, Father's friend wrote. He was finding gold every day. Next came two sentences that made Ready's heart leap: *Too bad you and your boy aren't here to help me, Henry. The work would go much faster.*

"I'll go," Ready blurted. "I can leave tomorrow!"

"Absolutely not," his mother replied and abruptly left the room.

Ready wouldn't drop the subject there. But he needed to lay some groundwork before he brought it up again. What if Mr. Seldon wrote a letter specifically requesting Ready's help? After mulling things over, he wrote to Father's friend explaining things. Maybe Mr. Seldon would see it as a way to help the Gates family in their time of need. He mailed the letter without telling anyone.

Ready wasn't the only one writing letters. On Frank Wyman's behalf, Lydia wrote to newspapers in Downieville and Placerville, explaining what had happened to the mail. She'd also arranged for small ads in those papers: *Mr. Joseph Peckham is urgently requested to contact his sister in care of the San Francisco Post Office.* It was a good idea. Ready wished he'd thought of it himself.

On May 21, Ready saw the outstretched signal arms on Telegraph Hill. Another sidewheel steamer with eastern newspapers had entered San Francisco Bay. Good, it had arrived early in the day. He could sell papers and still get home in time to help his brothers build the furnace in the back yard. They had been collecting cans for weeks now, but every time they planned to make solder, something had come up. His brothers were getting impatient. Ready had promised they'd finally do it tonight.

He reached the wharf in time to see the little Adams Express Company boat get the eastern papers from the *Northerner*. When the rowboat returned to the dock, the man with the papers shouted up to Ready, "Guess what? Lola Montez is on this ship!"

The news spread like wildfire through the waiting crowd. *Lola has come!* The Divine Lola. The celebrated actress and dancer. She'd been romanced by rich and famous men, including the king of Bavaria. Why, he'd even made her a countess! But oh, she had a world-famous temper, too. Once, she horsewhipped a man who'd insulted her. Imagine, Lola Montez, here in San Francisco.

For the first time ever, Ready had no takers for the *New York Herald*. All eyes focused on the approaching *Northerner*. The crowd hushed as the gangplank was set in place.

Ready recognized the first people off the ship. California Senator William Gwin. Wealthy San Francisco merchant Sam Brannan. And the ruddy-faced Irishman Patrick Hull, owner of the *San Francisco Whig*.

Pat Hull had given Ready his first newspaper job, one week after the Gates family had landed in San Francisco. Working as a "fly-boy" at the *Whig*—removing the newspapers from the press as they were printed—Ready had enjoyed listening to the editor's witty stories. But selling papers paid more. When a position opened up at the *Alta California*, Ready had left for greener pastures.

Mr. Hull strode confidently off the steamer, carrying a leather valise. His eyes lit up when he saw Ready. "Gates!

Still plying the newspaper trade, I see. Have we lost you permanently to the competition?"

Ready grinned. "I go where the money is, sir. Today, I've got the *New York Herald*." He lowered his voice. "Mr. Hull. Is it true Lola Montez is on board?"

The Irishman sighed. "True enough, my boy. And every man on the ship is in love with her. Watch that ramp. In a few minutes you'll see the most beautiful woman in the world walk down it." With a parting salute to Ready, Mr. Hull headed towards town.

The crowd gasped when a stunning woman dressed in black velvet appeared at the top of the gangway. Her dark hair framed a pale and delicate face, but there was nothing meek about her manner. She stood ramrod straight, surveying the crowd below like a queen viewing her subjects. Then, she strode boldly down the gangway, followed closely by a maid carrying a cocker spaniel.

Ready knew he should move out of the way, but his legs felt riveted to the spot. Mr. Hull was right. Lola Montez *was* the most beautiful woman in the world! Mesmerized, Ready watched her step off the plank and stop right in front of him. Why couldn't he move his feet?

Lola's violet eyes twinkled. Mustering his composure, Ready doffed his cap with a flourish and bowed. Then, impulsively, he took an orange from his pocket and presented it to her with great fanfare.

"Welcome to San Francisco, Countess."

Lola took the orange and rewarded him with a dazzling smile. "Well, aren't you a charming young fellow." Her accent sounded vaguely Spanish. "You must come see me dance."

Then, with an almost imperceptible twitch of her head, she signaled for Ready to move. This time he did. Sam Brannan materialized out of the crowd to escort Lola to a carriage. The maid followed with the dog. Close behind, porters carried more than thirty pieces of luggage, which they placed in a wagon. Then, Lola's carriage took off towards town.

After Lola's departure from the waterfront, things returned to normal, and Ready easily found customers for the *New York Herald*. He stopped for bread and then hurried home. If Father was awake, Ready would tell him about San Francisco's newest celebrity.

When he entered the kitchen, however, to his surprise, he found Lydia and his mother poring over Father's map of the gold region.

Lydia handed him a piece of paper. "A letter from Miss Emily."

Ready took it and read aloud:

"My dear Lydia: After I left you in San Francisco, my river trip to Marysville was blessedly uneventful. (I still shudder to remember our dreadful experience, and every day praise God that you and I were spared.) I found my brother Thomas and our store in good shape, though plenty of work awaited me. Therefore, it was several weeks before I returned to my usual task of inspecting our accounting books.

"How startled I was to see a notation for late March that listed the purchaser as "J. Peckham." I ran to my brother to see if he remembered that customer. Alas, he did not. It was a busy time at the store. Miners who had been snowbound for months were finally able to reach town for supplies.

"Thomas and I then inquired all over town for Mr. J. Peckham. He's not here, and no one remembers him. If this was your brother, as of late March, he was alive and still in California. I promise to keep my eyes and ears open, in case he passes this way again. Keep up your courage, dear girl, and know you are always welcome in my home. Yours truly, Emily Blake."

Lydia traced her finger on the map. "Frank Wyman traveled between Downieville and Placerville. Marysville is far to the west of that. It doesn't look like he would have even gone to Marysville."

Ready studied the area where her finger pointed. "But the Feather River flows from Downieville to Marysville. Joseph might have taken a boat there for supplies and then returned upriver to work a claim."

"If it's even the same J. Peckham," his mother answered pessimistically. "If it's even the same one."

The arrival of Lola Montez lit a new kind of fire in San Francisco. Shopkeepers put up special displays and labeled their wares "Lola Montez Fashions." A horse named Lola Montez came in first place at the Pioneer Race Course. And the town buzzed with gossip.

Everywhere Ready went, he heard something outrageous about Lola. That she bathed in lavender water and dried herself with rose petals. That her dog slept on a silk cushion and ate only filet mignon. That she smoked cigars, drank liquor, and carried a loaded pistol.

But while San Franciscans clucked their tongues, they clamored for a look at the countess. When it was announced that Lola would appear in a play at the American Theater, there was a mad rush for tickets. Though he knew his parents would disapprove of spending the money, Ready tried to buy a ticket for Lola's opening night. But, all two thousand seats were sold out.

"How about one for the next night?" he asked.

The man shook his head. "Come back tomorrow."

Determined not to miss out this time, Ready headed for the ticket office early the next day. As he passed by the office of the *San Francisco Whig*, Pat Hull called to him from the doorway.

"Ready Gates! May I have a moment of your time?"

The newspaperman led him to a back room and shut the door. "I know you're good at spreading the news, young man. But can you do the opposite? Can you keep a secret?"

"If the secret's worth keeping, sir."

Mr. Hull paced back and forth. Finally, he spoke. "I've been courting Lola Montez since I met her on board the *Northerner*."

Pat Hull and Lola Montez? Ready's face betrayed not a flicker of astonishment.

The Irishman continued to pace. "She wants to keep our friendship a secret until her performances here have run their course. I need your help to win her heart."

How could he help Mr. Hull romance Lola Montez? "Happy to oblige, sir."

"I need your services as a messenger. I'll pay you well. But I need your absolute assurance that anything you hear from me—or the Countess—will remain in strictest confidence." The editor stuck out his hand. "Deal?"

Ready returned the handshake. "Yes, sir." *But what about Sam Brannan?*

As if reading his mind, Mr. Hull said, "Lola likes being treated like royalty. Sam Brannan has showered her with expensive gifts since the steamer landed, including that horse and carriage she uses to take her dog to the beach. Brannan may be rich, but he's a sourpuss. Lola could never be happy with him. I make Lola laugh. Don't be fooled by that Spanish accent. She's as Irish as they come. She enjoys a good yarn like the best of us."

Hull stopped pacing. "I'm a journalist. Words are my weapon and my ally. Every day, I will write a letter, which you will deliver. I'll woo Lola with humor, drama, and Irish charm." He asked Ready to return at five p.m. for the first installment and a ticket for that night's performance.

With his brothers watching enviously, Ready took extra care with his appearance. He shined his shoes, scrubbed his fingernails, and put on his best shirt.

"Show us again," Hugh begged. "Show us again."

Ready pulled out the ticket Mr. Hull had given him. "Five dollars—dress circle. No cheap balcony seat for me tonight!"

The American Theatre was bigger and fancier than the Adelphi. A huge chandelier hung from an ornate ceiling. On each side of the stage, gilded eagles held smaller chandeliers in their beaks. As Ready settled into his plush red seat, he heard people talking about Lola's famous Spider Dance.

But as the lamps dimmed and the curtain opened, first came the play *Daemon and Pythias,* performed by the theater's resident actors. The audience, itching for Lola, shifted in their seats. Next came *Yelva*, a drama starring Lola as a

71

deaf-mute girl, delivering her lines in pantomime. People yawned. When the resident actors came back for another play, the audience grumbled.

Finally, it was time for the Spider Dance. Lola sailed onto stage in a brightly colored Spanish costume. She wore flesh-colored tights under layers of short skirts, giving the daring impression of bare legs. *Grandma would faint,* Ready thought. *Mother wouldn't like it much, either.* Red flowers encircled Lola's black hair. She floated gracefully across the stage. Then, the musicians played *La Tarantella*, and the Spider Dance began.

Lola whirled to the beat of the music, portraying a woman caught in a huge spider web. Then she discovered a spider in her petticoat, which she tried to shake loose with graceful leaps into the air. The web was left to the audience's imagination, but the spider was a stage prop as big as her hand. Suddenly, Lola shook her skirts violently, revealing a rainbow of petticoats infested with dozens of spiders, big and small.

The tempo sped up as the battle against the spiders intensified. As the music reached its final crescendo, Lola shook all of the spiders out upon the floor and stomped them flat. The audience erupted into thunderous applause. She smiled radiantly and glided from stage, carefully avoiding the smashed carcasses of fake spiders.

Ready darted out a side exit and hurried around the back to the stage door. A guard blocked his way.

"I have an urgent message for Mademoiselle Montez!"

The doorman didn't budge.

Ready tried the code phrase Mr. Hull had given him. "It's a message for Eliza from the Irish chap."

The man stepped aside. "Turn left at the hallway, second door on the right."

The password had worked. Lola was expecting him. As Ready peeked cautiously down the hall, a voice from behind startled him.

"Does the orange-headed boy bring another orange?"

He spun around to find Lola still dressed in her Spanish costume. She held a bouquet of roses in one hand and a cork spider in the other.

"Countess." Ready bowed. "You were *magnificent*."

Lola flashed a smile and spoke with a heavy accent. "My first impression was correct. You *are* a charming boy."

She led him into the dressing room and pointed to a table laden with flowers, fruit and cakes. "Boys are always hungry. Eat, while I change out of my costume."

He didn't even flinch when she called him a boy. He took a piece of cake. If only Max could see him now!

Lola stepped behind an ornate screen. She emerged moments later in a red silk dressing gown and a necklace of sparkling rubies. "Don't you have a message for me?"

She took the sealed letter from his hand, tossed it carelessly on the dressing table, and said in unaccented English, "I'll read it later. You run along now."

CHAPTER ELEVEN

Pat Hull persuaded Ready to leave the *Alta California* and sell the *Whig* instead. Now, when his papers were gone, he'd drop by the newspaper office to collect a sealed envelope for Lola and a ticket to that night's show. Although his mother did not approve of his spending so much time in entertainment halls, the extra money Mr. Hull paid him was welcome indeed.

For the moment, Ready forgot about his letter to Marcus Seldon and his still unfulfilled promise to make solder with his brothers. He didn't think about gold, or finding Lydia's brother, or his family's problems. For the first time in ages, he simply had fun. He bragged to the other newsboys about seeing all of Lola's shows. He endlessly described every detail of the Spider Dance.

Once, at a benefit for the volunteer firemen, Lola changed roles and portrayed the tarantula. Ready gasped when she appeared on stage in a grotesque mask. Spreading out her hands and feet like a spider, she bounced furiously from one side of the stage to the other, as if weaving a terrible web.

Then suddenly, the music changed. Lola ripped off the mask, revealing herself as the beautiful captive caught in the spider's snare. Bravely fighting her way out of the web, she victoriously broke through the strands one by one. Then, with her delicate foot, she crushed hundreds of tiny spiders that fell from her skirts to the floor.

The audience exploded into a frenzy of clapping, foot stomping, whistling, and cheering. Some firemen tossed their hats upon the stage. Others threw bouquets of roses. Throngs of admirers poured into the aisles and through the doors towards the backstage entrance. Somehow, amidst the pandemonium, Ready managed to reach Lola and thrust Hull's envelope into her waiting hand.

Pat Hull's letters to Lola apparently worked. When her performances ended in mid-June, the countess allowed the Irishman to squire her about town. The newspaperman no longer needed Ready as a messenger. But Mr. Hull offered him another job.

"Keep selling our papers in the morning," he said, "and we'll put you to work around the office in the afternoon. Run errands, set type, learn to operate the press. Think of it as an apprenticeship."

"May I still sell the *New York Herald* when the steamers arrive?"

Mr. Hull laughed heartily. "I'm sure I couldn't keep you away from your precious *New York Herald*. Just nothing from our San Francisco competitors, understand?"

For the first time, Ready started thinking differently about staying in San Francisco. Maybe he had a future here after all. Maybe he even had a future in the newspaper business. After all, look at the adventurous life Pat Hull led—hobnobbing with important people, rubbing elbows with high society, courting a beautiful woman. Maybe there were other ways to strike gold, instead of standing knee-deep in an icy stream.

A few days later, Ready stayed past supper time at the newspaper office, learning how to set type. Suddenly, the *Whig's* theater critic burst through the door.

"Doc Robinson opens a new show tonight called *Who's Got the Countess?*" He gave a devilish grin. "Any guesses?"

All the men laughed. Ready knew "Doc Robinson" was a popular comedian in San Francisco, but had never seen him perform.

The critic took a fistful of tickets from his pocket. "Why don't you join us, Ready? It should prove *educational*." The men laughed again.

"The typesetting lesson can wait," the pressman told Ready. "You go along with the others."

Doc Robinson began the satire with a song poking fun at Lola Montez, referred to in the play as "Mula, Countess of Bohemia." Mula was portrayed as a tempestuous, self-centered actress who couldn't remember her lines. But the funniest part of the show came when the actor known as "Uncle Billy" bounced out on stage in a Spanish dress, shaking out spiders as he went. The audience roared its approval. Feeling somewhat disloyal to Lola, Ready none-theless laughed until tears rolled down his cheeks and he began to hiccup.

On Friday, July 1, a young woman approached Ready while he was selling newspapers. *"Monsieur Gates?"*

Ready recognized Lola's French maid. *"Bonjour, made-moiselle."*

The maid slipped him a five-dollar gold piece. "Meet Mademoiselle Lola in the lobby of the Russ House at three o'clock," she whispered. "She will carry a red rose. Tell no one." Then she sped off.

Ready was mystified. A rose? Did Lola think he wouldn't recognize her? Why the secrecy?

He reached the Russ House a little before three. In one corner of the lobby, two men loudly discussed city politics. In another, a stout woman with a widow's black veil over her face dozed in a chair. No sign of Lola.

Ready sat down. After about ten minutes, the arguing men departed. No one else appeared. Had he misunderstood the time? Or had Lola changed her mind?

As Ready tapped his foot, the plump lady in black stood up and shuffled towards him. To his amazement, she dropped a red rose on his lap and sat down next to him.

"I thought they'd never leave."

The muffled voice was Lola's, without the Spanish accent. She handed Ready a slip of paper. *Madame de Cassins,* it said. *304 Dupont Street.* "Take me there," she whispered.

The gypsy? She'll probably say the countess has had a long and difficult journey. But, knowing Lola would tip him well, Ready happily obliged. "Grandma," he said loudly. "Let's go out and enjoy the sunshine!"

Lola stayed in character all the way to Dupont Street. Walking with a stoop, she stepped carefully along the wooden sidewalks, leaning her ample girth against her cane. At intersections, Ready gallantly helped her cross the street. At one point, they passed Max. He greeted Ready, glanced curiously at the old woman, and moved on.

At Madame de Cassins' house, the Chinese servant ushered them into the fortuneteller's presence. "You have traveled a great distance, Grandmother," she said. "You are troubled."

Lola removed her hat and veil, revealing her young appearance and curly black hair. Madame de Cassins peered silently at the famous face.

"You disguised your youth and beauty to come here. This was wise." Madame cast a dubious eye at Ready. "*Senorita,* I have a separate room where you and I may speak freely."

Left alone in the parlor, Ready perched impatiently on a carved wooden chair and then hopped up to examine an Egyptian parchment on the wall. When he leaned over to inspect it more closely, he detected muffled talking from the next room. Hoping the servant wouldn't catch him at it, Ready pressed his ear firmly against the wall and listened.

Lola was furious about *Who's Got the Countess?*, which had been playing to packed houses. She said that after all her generosity, she did not deserve to be mocked like this. Hadn't her benefit performance raised thousands of dollars for the fire department? San Franciscans should give her respect, not ridicule. Should she stay and fight for her honor? Or leave for her planned theatrical tour of the mining region?

Lola had other troubles as well. Her beloved spaniel, Flora, had disappeared. She had hired two detectives, but no trace of the dog could be found. And what should be done about Pat Hull, who kept pestering her to marry him?

"He's a charming man and utterly devoted to me," she

said. "Part of me wants to settle down as his wife in a cozy little house in the country. But the rest of me...."

At that moment, someone knocked at the front door. Ready leapt back into his chair just before the servant returned to answer it. He longed to hear Madame's answers to Lola, but it was not to be. When the Chinese man finally closed the door, the gypsy and Lola returned to the parlor.

"The young lady," Madame said to Ready. "Has she found her brother?"

"No. But we think he's somewhere between Downieville and Placerville."

Madame de Cassins reached over and fingered Ready's lapel. Then she withdrew her hand and placed it on her forehead, closing her eyes and breathing deeply. After a moment, she spoke. "She will find him. But only after you, my friend, have had a most unusual journey."

Most unusual? Ready thought. *Not long and difficult?* He smiled politely and followed Lola out the door.

That night, Ready finally had time to help his brothers tackle the supply of tin cans they had amassed over the past month. As they built a makeshift furnace, Charles asked Ready about plans for the upcoming Fourth of July.

"There's to be a balloon ascension," Charles said.

"Please take us, please," Hugh pleaded.

Ready shook his head. "I heard at the *Whig* today that the balloon was damaged in shipment. It won't be fixed in time for the Fourth."

When Hugh pouted in disappointment, Ready tried to cheer him up. "But Captain John Sutter himself will be leading a militia parade near the plaza. And there's sure to be fireworks."

Hugh and Charles seemed satisfied with that and returned to the task at hand. After several failed attempts, the boys finally figured out what to do. First, they put the cans in the fire till the molten solder trickled down into the ashes like quicksilver. After it cooled, they collected up the misshapen lumps and placed them in an old skillet. Then they re-melted the lumps and poured the pig lead into molds made from cake tins. When they were done, they had several pounds of it.

"Take it to the metalsmith tomorrow," Ready told his brothers. "Let's see how much money he gives you."

The boys carefully extinguished the flames in the back yard, not wanting to start yet another San Francisco fire. As they finished up, a messenger from the *Whig* arrived at the Gates house.

"I was told to give you this." He handed Ready a note and then left.

Ready opened the note. *6 a.m. Saturday, Mission Dolores. Tell no one. L.M.* He reread the message with exasperation. Six a.m. at the Mission? Why? Would they read tea leaves together? Or look for her missing dog? Surely, she wouldn't marry Pat Hull at that place and hour. It would be Lola's style to book the American Theater and hold a parade, as well.

His curiosity piqued, Ready arose before five for the long walk down the plank road. At first, he saw no one. But as he neared the Mission, several carriages passed him. When he reached the courtyard of the church, he recognized several local dignitaries. Another carriage rolled up.

Out stepped Pat Hull in a morning coat and top hat, followed by Lola in a gray silk dress and bonnet. She winked at Ready.

He followed the group into the church and sat in the back. Lola walked down the aisle carrying a vase of white silk roses, which she placed in front of a statue of the Virgin Mary. Then Lola Montez and Pat Hull exchanged wedding vows. Ready paid strict attention. Max would want to know every detail.

CHAPTER TWELVE

For several days, Ready basked in the glory of being one of the few people in town to have witnessed the marriage of Lola Montez. He'd even attended the wedding breakfast and had waved good-bye when the bride and groom had left town by riverboat. It wasn't just Max and the other newsboys who asked about it. Reporters from the *Whig* and the *Alta California* pressed him for details of what the bride had worn, what food had been served, and what might have been said about Lola's future plans.

All Ready knew was that Lola had decided to take her Spider Dance to Sacramento and points beyond.

"What about Pat Hull?" the reporters asked.

Ready could only shrug.

While still glowing from his new-found notoriety, Ready received a letter from Marcus Seldon. Father's friend had taken on a new partner at Agua Fria Creek and therefore didn't need Ready's help. On a different day, Ready would have felt bitterly disappointed. But now, it only made him yearn more forcefully for Pat Hull's return. He wanted to get started in earnest on that promised apprenticeship.

No one at the *Whig* knew anything more, either. Hull had given no instructions for his absence. The paper didn't publish on Sunday, July 3, or Monday, Independence Day. As promised, Ready took his brothers to see the July Fourth festivities at the plaza.

At ten o'clock, the National Lancers started the parade. Forty young men in smart blue uniforms proudly rode their horses down Kearny Street. They were followed by dozens of other militia groups from around the state, banners fluttering in the stiff breeze. When all troops were in position, John Sutter rode up to City Hall on a horse and dismounted. Just as the well-known pioneer climbed the steps to the reviewing platform, there was a big commotion on the sidewalk behind him.

Someone had lobbed a lit firecracker into a store selling fireworks. It landed in the middle of a huge bin of rockets, setting off a chain reaction of explosions. The store was suddenly engulfed in flames, as panicked people fled in all directions. Ready and his brothers ducked down an alley way to avoid being trampled by the crowd.

Somehow, the Empire One Fire Company made it through the chaotic streets and extinguished the flames. Then, the California Guard fired a thirty-two gun salute, and John Sutter and his military battalion paraded out of Portsmouth Square.

The next day, Ready returned home to find Lydia sitting on the front porch with his brothers.

"Look what was waiting for me at the post office!" She handed Ready a small leather case. Inside was a daguerreotype likeness of a lanky young man sporting a full beard. The fellow's nose was bent to one side, as if it had once been broken.

Ready's jaw dropped. "Is this your brother?"

She nodded, grinning. "Read this."

Taking the letter, he read aloud:

*Dearest Cousin Lydia: This parcel and letter arrived some time after your message explaining about your ordeal with the In-*dependence. *We are relieved to learn you are well, and by reading the enclosed letter, that Joseph is well, too. We pray you find each other soon. Love, Cousin Mildred and family.*

Lydia handed Ready another letter, which he also read aloud:

March 28, 1853. My dearest Sissy Lid: I send you the enclosed likeness, since it will probably be a long time before you see me in person. I have just experienced a most horrendous winter. I spent four months trapped by snow in a miner's cabin near the North Fork of the Yuba River. I probably could have gotten myself out, but my friend and mining partner, Alpha Crippen, was deathly ill. I couldn't very well leave him alone, so there I stayed.

What dreary hours we spent in that cabin, buried by twenty feet of snow. I dug a hole from the door to the surface, so I could occasionally climb out and look around.

After our provisions ran out, I managed to shoot a deer. We feasted for days. Later, when food ran low again, I boiled those bones till they shone like polished ivory.

Eventually, Alpha felt better, and enough snow melted for us to leave. I left him with friends in Downieville. Then I found my way to Marysville, some eighty miles to the south. There, I chanced upon the traveling daguerreotypist who made this portrait. It turned out the man needed an assistant and hired me immediately.

So, dear sister, as you sit comfortably in Aunt Clarissa's parlor studying this face, know that its owner is tramping around the wilds of California, making likenesses of homesick miners to send to their families. I'll write when I can. All my love to you, Aunt Clarissa and the cousins.

Your brother, Joseph Peckham.

PS. I'll mail this in Auburn, but keep sending my letters to San Francisco. I suppose letters from you are waiting for me even now. I'll send for them when I can. Keep writing.

Ready grabbed Lydia's hands and spun her around the porch. Hugh and Charles joined in, and soon the four of them collapsed in a heap of laughter. Ready thought Lydia's beaming face seemed more beautiful than ever. He felt a funny little tug at his heart and his cheeks burned. No one else noticed, however. His brothers scrutinized Joseph Peckham's picture, asking Lydia about every detail.

Then, Ready remembered something. "Lydia, I met a traveling daguerreotypist in Sacramento!" He told her about the man who had bought his newspapers.

"How many portrait takers could there be in the gold region?"

"I don't know. But this man said he'd just hired an assistant. And he was staying near Marysville. Lydia, it has to be the same one!"

"Do you remember his name?"

At first, Ready could not. Then, he remembered the image the man had shown him, of a wagon that looked like a house. It came to him. *"Wallace's Daguerrian Saloon.* The man's name was Clarence Wallace."

"How do we find him?"

"I don't know. But we have more to go on than we did before."

Ready took another look at the likeness of Joseph Peckham. "Your brother looks like you, Lydia. He has the same kind, intelligent eyes. I suspect that under that beard of his, he has the same determined jaw."

Just then, Horace Fitz came walking down the street towards the house. Lydia jumped up and ran to him. "Horace! You'll never guess what was waiting at the post office today!"

As Ready watched Lydia talking and laughing with Horace, he felt the same stabs of jealousy he'd felt at the theater weeks before. He turned to his brothers. "Come on, boys. Mother must need our help with something."

The following Monday, as Ready returned from selling newspapers, he spied Pat Hull stepping into a carriage outside the *Whig* office. Ready was a block away at the time.

"Mr. Hull," he shouted, breaking into a run. "Mr. Hull!"

The Irishman didn't appear to hear him. Before Ready could reach it, the carriage disappeared around a corner.

Inside the newspaper office, Ready learned that Pat Hull had just sold the *Whig*. The new owners would rename it the *Commercial Advertiser*. Ready could sell papers if he liked, but nothing more. His apprenticeship had ended before it even began.

CHAPTER THIRTEEN

The summer dragged on. Father's recovery was excruciatingly slow. Mother continued to sew, with Lydia's help. Though it didn't pay much, his brothers kept collecting cans for pig lead. Ready felt more frustrated with each passing day.

Initially, he had hoped to distinguish himself with his new bosses at the *Commercial Advertiser* by selling more papers than anyone else. Unfortunately, news was slow. Boys selling the *Alta California* and the *San Francisco Herald* had no better luck. The only time any newsboy earned decent money was when a steamer brought the *New York Herald*.

So, it was back to finding odd jobs. Running errands and delivering produce. Carrying packages. Distributing handbills for upcoming theater shows. If all else failed, he'd collect cans for his brothers.

As Ready raced about town doing whatever paying work he could find, he often daydreamed about finding Lydia's brother. The dreams usually included Lydia flinging her arms around Ready in undying gratitude, but never spelled out how Ready would actually find Joseph Peckham. He'd have to locate Clarence Wallace, first. But how?

One day, as he walked by a portrait gallery on Clay Street, Ready had an idea. Maybe someone here would know something about Wallace's Daguerrian Saloon. He went inside and spoke to the proprietor.

The man paused to think. "Wallace might have bought supplies from me once. Short fellow, isn't he?"

Ready nodded. "Do you know how I might find him?"

"Hard to say." The daguerreotypist fingered his whiskers thoughtfully. "There are a number of these traveling dag artists. Some bring their equipment into town and rent space in a hotel. Others, like your Clarence Wallace, have their own traveling galleries. Some advertise in the local newspapers. Others just post a sign and wait for word to get around. They'll do as much business as they can in a week or so and then move on."

Ready thanked the man and mulled over this new information. There must be a way to track down Clarence Wallace. Maybe another advertisement? Lydia had spent a lot of money on ads already, with no result. Wait a minute. The man said the dag artists *themselves* bought ads. Ready suddenly took off running.

That evening, he returned home with an armload of newspapers.

"What's this?" Hugh demanded, as Ready dumped them all over the bed.

"Reading material," Ready said. "The *Shasta Courier*. The *Marysville Express*. The *Sonora Herald*."

"Where did they come from?"

"The *Commercial Advertiser* receives newspapers from all over California. When the editors are done with them, they throw them out."

"Why do you want them?"

Ready grinned. "They're going to help me find Wallace's Daguerrian Saloon."

That night, Ready pored over the papers by lamplight. He learned which boarding houses caught fire, which creeks overflowed their banks, and which editors disliked Governor John Bigler. But he found no mention of any daguerreotypist, anywhere.

The next day, Ready brought home more papers. The *Calaveras Chronicle*. The *Nevada Journal*. Finally, in the *Downieville Mountain Echo*, he found this item:

DAGUERREOTYPIST Lewis Whitney is happy to announce to the ladies and gentlemen of Downieville and vicinity that he is now prepared to execute likenesses in the highest perfection of the art. Rooms in the Carter House. As he will remain in town but a short time, persons wishing their portraits are solicited to call as soon as convenient.

These traveling dag artists *did* advertise. If Ready kept looking, he was sure to find Clarence Wallace. He wrote a letter to Brother Brewster in Placerville, and to the editors of several newspapers—explaining his search for the daguerreotypist and asking for help in locating him.

The next time Lydia came over to the Gates house, Ready showed her the newspapers.

"I'll take some of them home with me," she said. "Maybe the ladies at Mrs. Salem's will help me look through them."

Ready agreed to drop more papers off at Mrs. Salem's every few days. "With all of us looking," Ready assured her, "it's only a matter of time."

One day, Doc Robinson hired Ready and Max to hand out ads for his newest show, *The Past, Present and Future of San Francisco*. In addition to a little cash, he gave them each a free ticket. Ready was delighted.

While the play claimed to be historical drama, it was in fact, Doc Robinson's characteristic satire. His parodies of current events and local politicians drew as much raucous laughter as *Who's Got the Countess?* had two months earlier. At one point, when Ready and Max were laughing so much they almost fall out of their seats, Ready happened to spot a familiar-looking man across the theater. Ready didn't think much about it, since he met so many people in San Francisco each day. Yet, later, when the audience stood up to leave, Ready noticed the man again, and how much shorter he was than the people around him. Suddenly, Ready realized why the man looked familiar. It was Clarence Wallace, the daguerreotypist!

Ready caught up with him outside the theater. "Excuse me, sir. I must speak with you!"

Mr. Wallace turned around. "Yes?"

"I've been searching for you. Do you remember me? I sold you a stack of *Boston Journals* in a Sacramento saloon."

Mr. Wallace gave a look of surprised recognition. "Why have you been looking for me?"

Ready's words rushed out in a jumble. "You told me you had just hired a new assistant. Is he a tall man named Joseph Peckham?"

"No. He's a short man named Carl Sprague."

Ready felt like someone had punched him hard in the stomach. He had been so sure Clarence Wallace was the key to finding Joseph Peckham, he would have staked his life on it. All those hours of reading tiny newsprint by candlelight, all those letters he'd sent out—for naught!

The daguerreotypist steered Ready towards a crate on the sidewalk. "Why don't you sit here and catch your breath?"

Regaining his composure, Ready explained the situation. Mr. Wallace listened sympathetically. "Even if I hadn't shown up today, it sounds like you would have tracked me down before long. Too bad I'm not the one you really want."

The daguerreotypist paused. "But I might be able to help you. When I returned to Marysville, my assistant told me an old friend of mine had stopped by in my absence. A dag artist named Hezekiah Waldow. That would have been about the time your fellow was in Marysville."

"Did Waldow hire an assistant?"

"I don't know. I never saw him. However, I'm sure he could use one. He doesn't have a saloon on wheels like mine. He actually has his own building, made so that he can take it completely apart and transport it by wagon. When he comes to a town, he finds a vacant lot and sets up his gallery in two hours. Ingenious contraption it is."

Ready felt the flicker of hope rekindling. "How might I *find* Hezekiah Waldow?"

The daguerreotypist shrugged. "He could be anywhere. If I were you, I'd keep reading those newspapers. He's bound to buy an ad sooner or later."

CHAPTER FOURTEEN

In August, San Francisco bricklayers went on strike. With no one buying bricks, the factory laid off its workers, including Horace Fitz and other boarders at the Gates house. Other tradesmen went on strike, too. This had a ripple effect. Many people were out of work.

While trying to think up new ways to earn money, Ready spotted an announcement in the *Commercial Advertiser:*

GRAND BALLOON ASCENSION
FROM CONTRA COSTA
ON SUNDAY, 28TH AUGUST
The Mammoth Balloon CALIFORNIA, the largest ever constructed in America, and when inflated capable of carrying
THREE PERSONS,
Will ascend from Contra Costa on Sunday, August 28th, under the personal superintendence of Messrs. Kelly & Goodell. About 1 o'clock P.M., Mr. Kelly will leave terra firma for the upper regions, accompanied by a lady, which will doubtless be the most magnificent spectacle ever witnessed in California. Such arrangements have been made with the Contra Costa Ferry Company, of which due notice will be given as will afford to all who wish, an opportunity of witnessing this sublime spectacle.

Ready showed the ad to Max.

"Sounds fun," Max replied.

"More than fun," Ready said. "A way to earn money!"

"How?"

"It's San Francisco's first balloon ascension. Hundreds of people will go. Maybe thousands! Let's sell something."

"Peanuts?"

Ready shook his head. "The fruit vendor I work for just received a huge shipment of oranges. I'm sure he'd give us a good price. When all those people get hot and thirsty, we could probably sell them for a dollar apiece."

Max grimaced. "Peanuts are lighter to carry."

"We'll make more money with oranges."

In the end, Max agreed.

Ready found Lydia washing supper dishes at Mrs. Salem's. "I brought you some more newspapers."

"Keep your tiresome papers," Lydia answered crossly.

Ready raised his eyebrows. "What's wrong?"

Lydia flung the dishrag into the basin so hard, it splashed water on the floor. "We've chased shadows for months!" she wailed. "Buying ads. Putting our hopes on a letter that went up in smoke. Putting out our eyes reading the fine print in a never-ending stack of newspapers—looking for the wrong person!"

"That was before," Ready said. "Now we know Hezekiah Waldow was in Marysville the same time as your brother. He must be the one."

"Maybe," she replied coldly. "In any event, I may not be around to read newspapers with you anymore."

"What do you mean?"

"Horace asked me to marry him. He's leaving for Oregon and wants me to accompany him as his wife."

Ready tried not to show his dismay. "What did you tell him?"

"That I needed time to think about such a big decision."

"I hope you say no."

"Oh, you *do*." Lydia's eyes flashed. "You think I should toss away what may be my only chance for a decent life? Shall I grow old scrubbing floors in a boarding house, reading the Downieville *Mountain Echo* in my spare time?"

"Lydia, you're sixteen," Ready said. "This isn't your only chance for a decent life. You came to California to be with your brother. Remember your plans to travel and maybe start a store together? Shouldn't you wait until we find him?"

"I don't think we're ever going to!" Lydia burst into sobs.

Ready awkwardly placed his hand on her arm. "But now we know the name of the man Joseph works for."

She brushed his hand away. "Maybe we do and maybe we don't. *And we're no closer to finding him anyway.*" She wiped her eyes with the dish towel.

"Horace is a good man, Lydia," Ready said. "But if you marry him, shouldn't it be for *himself*, not because you can't find your brother?"

Lydia glowered at Ready and stomped off, slamming the door behind her.

Sunday morning, Ready and Max bought as many oranges as they could carry in two large canvas bags and caught the ten o'clock ferry. Across the bay, the hills of Contra Costa that had looked so green in spring were now faded to a golden brown. As the ferryboat approached its destination, Ready reminded himself this new town was now called Oakland. Though most San Franciscans still referred to it as Contra Costa.

The boys followed the crowd to a small yard on Third Street. A huge yellow silk balloon lay spread out on the ground, connected by a hose to a gas-making apparatus. A rigging of knotted cords surrounded the balloon, as if someone had flung a large fishing net around it. This rigging was tied to a wooden hoop, about three feet wide, underneath the balloon. Eventually, a big wicker basket would be attached to the hoop. For now, it sat off to one side. Ready peeked in it and saw sandbags, blankets, and a picnic hamper. Provisions for the trip?

The men fumbling with the gas-making machine appeared to be having problems. It wasn't hard to pick out the aeronaut, Mr. Kelly. He paced back and forth nervously, barking instructions. Ready saw no sign of the lady who was supposed to go along for the ride.

Ready and Max staked out a spot under a tree. While one stood guard over the oranges, the other could explore Oakland. In an hour, they had seen everything the small town had to offer. The crowd had now grown to well over a thousand people, and the ferries continued to bring more. Yet, the balloon remained only partially filled.

"Walk around and admire the scenery, folks!" Mr. Kelly stood on a box and shouted at the crowd through his speaking trumpet. "The balloon won't leave until one o'clock."

But it didn't leave at one. And it didn't leave at two. The ferryboats brought more people, and the day grew hotter. Still the balloon sat only partly inflated.

Periodically, Mr. Kelly reassured the crowd through his speaking trumpet. "Just a little while longer, folks. A little while longer."

About two-thirty, Mr. Kelly launched two small, unmanned balloons, just to give people something to look at. As they floated up and disappeared from sight, Ready heard grumbling everywhere he turned. *This aeronaut is a fraud. He's wasting our time. I'm hot. I'm thirsty. Let's go home.*

At three, Ready and Max started selling their oranges. As they moved through the crowd, Ready heard people shouting insults at the aeronaut. Mopping his face with a handkerchief, Mr. Kelly finally announced it was time. Ready scurried back with his remaining oranges and stood as close to the balloon as he could. It looked about two-thirds full.

The men fastened the basket to the balloon's hoop and Mr. Kelly climbed in. Someone untied the mooring rope and the balloon began to move—sideways along the street, not up in the air.

"I told you it wouldn't work," a voice heckled. "He doesn't know what he's doing!"

"Just a moment, folks!" Mr. Kelly shouted. "These things take time."

The aeronaut climbed out, and a smaller man climbed in. The decrease in weight helped slightly, and the balloon rose about two feet. Then, it lurched sideways again. The basket bumped along the street until it came to rest against a tree. Mr. Kelly ran after it. Ready followed right behind.

Mr. Kelly said, "We must lighten the load. Remove the basket."

The men detached the basket and lashed a four-inch-wide board across the middle of the hoop. A smaller man sat on the board. The balloon rose about six feet and then stopped.

The grumbling resumed. *This balloon isn't going anywhere. This fellow doesn't know what he's doing. When is that next ferry-boat home, anyway?*

Finally, someone shouted, "Let a boy try it!"

"Yes, a boy!" others exclaimed. The crowd took up the chant. "A boy. A boy. A boy!"

Ready's eyes lit up. Ride a balloon? He'd love to. He handed his oranges and money pouch to Max. "I'll do it. Let me!"

The crowd parted and Ready strode purposely to the balloon. He straddled the plank the way he'd sat on a hobbyhorse as a young child, letting his legs dangle below him. He grasped the thin ropes attaching the balloon to the hoop and called to Max, "Save me an orange in case I get thirsty."

Mr. Kelly showed him a rope hanging from the top of the balloon. "Pull this valve cord when you want to come down."

Someone released the mooring rope and the balloon rose about ten feet in the air. The people clapped and cheered as a gentle breeze pushed it horizontally. Beaming down at the sea of upturned faces, Ready laughed with delight.

Then a sharp gust of wind grabbed the balloon and Ready saw the ground fall away. He was rising quickly!

His heart thumped against his chest as the shrieking crowd looked smaller and smaller.

Mr. Kelly's voice boomed through the speaking trumpet. *"Pull the valve cord!"*

Ready seized it and pulled. Nothing happened. He pulled harder. To his horror, it broke off in his hand. As he stared in disbelief at the frayed rope, the earth below fell farther and farther away.

CHAPTER FIFTEEN

Though he couldn't actually feel the balloon moving, Ready could tell he was rising rapidly. Fear clawed at the pit of his stomach. He felt dizzy and cold. He closed his eyes and hung on tight. Like before in the engine room, the only prayer that came to mind was, "Deliver us from evil." He whispered those words fiercely now. *Deliver us from evil. Deliver us from evil.*

He opened his eyes. He didn't seem to be rising any more for the moment. He forced himself to breath slowly and calmly. In and out. In and out.

Suddenly, the balloon spun quickly around, almost bucking Ready off. His heart hammered as he squeezed his legs around the wooden plank and clung even tighter to the ropes. He felt sick to his stomach. Finally, things settled down. Now he was drifting east.

Despite his fear, Ready marveled at the amazing panorama below him. To the west, San Francisco Bay looked like a pond filled with toy boats. He saw Goat Island, Angel Island, Alcatraz. Beyond the bay, in the city itself, he picked out Telegraph Hill and Long Wharf. He saw a tiny vessel entering the bay. *Side-wheel steamer.* Here he was, first to spot the mail ship! What good did it do him? Across the

Golden Gate, that cluster of boats and waterfront buildings had to be Sausalito. And far, far to the north, that solitary snowy peak. Could it be Mount Shasta?

Ready pondered his predicament. How long would this thing stay up? Would he float for days? What if the wind blew him out to sea? What if the balloon hurled him to the depths below? *Would he ever see his family again?*

Tears stung his eyes as he pictured his loved ones. Father, still bedridden. Mother, working hard all day, quietly reading her Bible at night. Could her prayers save him now? Charles and Hugh. Were they watching the balloon from a distant rooftop? And Lydia, soon-to-be-married Lydia. He'd fancied himself her rescuer. Now, he couldn't even save himself.

Ready studied the yellow silk monster above him. The neck of the balloon pointed straight down, wide open. Shouldn't the men have tied it closed to keep the gas from escaping? But, no. Gas was lighter than air. It wouldn't leak out an opening at the bottom of the balloon. But what about one on the side or the top?

He felt for the penknife in his pocket. Could he possibly climb up and poke a hole in the balloon? And if he did, would the gas rush out, dropping him from the sky like a shot bird? He didn't think so. A small tear should let the gas leak out slowly.

But could he get up high enough to make a useful hole? He scrutinized the balloon and its ropes. Could he climb up, squeeze himself between the netting and the balloon, and worm his way even higher?

A voice from below startled him. *"Ho, balloooooooooon."*

Ready peered at the landscape below, trying to see who had called out. A Sunday hiker? He was passing over Mount Diablo, a peak he'd often spotted on the steamboat from Sacramento. It was now only a blurred mass below him. He waved anyway, grateful for the brief human contact.

The wind shifted, pushing him northwesterly. Shivering from both anxiety and the cold, Ready took his bearings again. He could see the mouth of the Sacramento River. He floated high above the town of Martinez. He distinctly saw people in the streets—*they looked like ants!*—and a steamboat at the wharf. Did anyone below notice him?

Across the channel from Martinez stood Benicia, the state capital. To the east, boats plied the Sacramento River. Much farther east, rose the towering peaks of the Sierra Nevada.

The balloon continued to climb higher, as it headed north over the marshes of Suisun Bay. The loftier height was both exhilarating and more frightening. What would happen if he went too high? What if he kept going north into sparsely populated territory? Even if he landed safely, he might end up as food for grizzly bears! The time had come for action.

He opened his knife and placed it in his teeth. He cautiously raised himself to a crouch on the plank. So far, so good. The balloon held steady.

Slowly, he slid his hands up the ropes, trying to reach the netting. But the thin cords—only a quarter-inch wide—cut at his hands whenever he tested his weight against them. Could he hoist himself up to the netting and climb it?

After struggling with the ropes for several minutes, he gave up on his plan. The cords were too thin. Discouraged, he lowered himself back to a sitting position and put away the knife. He licked the rope burn on his palm and contemplated his next move.

As he gazed at the rolling plains beneath him and the hills beyond, Ready realized he had run out of familiar landmarks. However, he did spot a farmhouse, the only building for miles around.

Ready started shivering uncontrollably. His feet felt like ice. How could he get warm? He had a kerchief around his neck. Would that help? Carefully, he removed his right shoe, tied the kerchief around his foot and ankle, and put his shoe back on. It helped a little.

As he wondered how to warm up his other foot, the balloon began to spin rapidly. Clutching the ropes desperately, he again felt dizzy and nauseated. He must have hit some crosscurrents of air. Closing his eyes helped. Finally, despite his queasiness, he opened his eyes. The ground below seemed closer than before.

Looking up, he saw the balloon had twisted around inside the netting, probably from the spinning. The neck opening, previously pointed downward, had migrated to the side. It must be releasing gas! The balloon was quickly losing altitude. He was headed back to *terra firma*.

Ready anxiously watched the earth below rush closer and closer. Was he descending too fast? Could he do anything to break his fall? If not, would he crash and die, alone in this desolate area? He closed his eyes. *Deliver us from evil. Deliver us from evil.*

He opened his eyes. The balloon had reached a point about fifteen feet above the ground and stopped, momentarily motionless.

Not wanting to shoot back up into the sky, Ready prepared to jump. But suddenly, the balloon dropped like a rock. He landed hard on his right ankle and then found himself being dragged along the ground in a tangle of ropes.

Afraid the wind might lift him into the air again, he seized his knife and frantically sawed at the nearest cord. Twigs and rocks scraped at him as he bounced through the scrubby vegetation. He managed to cut one rope, then another.

The balloon continued to tow Ready on its horizontal journey across the hillside. Finally, a third line gave way. As he tumbled free from the balloon's clutches, it drifted upward once more.

"Ho, balloon," Ready muttered. "Good riddance."

Overwhelmed and exhausted, he lay on the ground shaking and sobbing. As the late afternoon sun gently warmed him, the numbness gradually left his hands and feet. Wiping his eyes on his sleeve, he sat up and took stock of his situation.

His ankle hurt, but he could walk on it. He had cuts, scrapes and rope burns. His left knee showed through a gash in his trousers. But, he had survived his voyage remarkably well. Now what?

From the sun, Ready figured it was about six o'clock. He'd been airborne more than two hours. He ran his tongue around his parched mouth. Too bad he didn't have an orange. Well, no use staying here. Where was that farmhouse he'd spotted earlier? South of here, he knew that.

He started walking. Could he find the house before nightfall? He climbed a hill to get his bearings. All around him, he saw only rolling fields of wild oats. No roads, no fences, certainly no buildings. He headed south. Even if he missed the farmhouse, he'd reach the bay eventually.

As he walked, he thought again of his family. Surely, Max would go straight to Ready's parents. *They'd all think he was dead.* It hurt to imagine how his parents must be feeling right now.

An hour later, Ready saw cultivated farmland ahead. He quickened his pace. Then he saw a small square on the horizon, barely noticeable in the twilight. Despite his tender ankle, he broke into a run. A gray-haired woman in a calico dress answered his knock and looked at him most curiously.

CHAPTER SIXTEEN

The following morning, Mrs. Thompson served Ready a heaping plate of griddlecakes. "If you're walking to Benicia, you need a good breakfast."

"Yes, ma'am." Ready eagerly helped himself. "Thank you, ma'am."

"Promise me you'll go immediately to your mother. She must be worried sick."

"Yes, ma'am."

"If you see Mr. Kelly again, tell him from me he has no business placing a boy like you at risk of life and limb."

"Yes, ma'am."

Mrs. Thompson gave Ready two apples and a piece of cornbread for later and pointed him towards Benicia. "You'll find the main road up there in a mile or so." She shook her head. "Mr. Thompson will never believe me when he returns. Imagine. A redheaded boy falling out of the sky. Why, I wouldn't believe that story myself."

Ready walked for several hours before a farmer in a wagon gave him a ride. Like Mrs. Thompson, at first the man did not believe him. However, Ready provided so many details the man finally accepted his word.

"Why didn't you hang on to the balloon after you landed?"

Ready laughed. "I'd held onto the blasted thing long enough."

At Benicia, the farmer dropped Ready off at First Street and pointed him towards the wharf. "The steamer from Sacramento should be along by nightfall."

Though he'd passed by it many times, Ready had never visited Benicia. Now, he studied the assortment of hotels, saloons, and stores. Where could he get something to drink? Too bad he'd left his money pouch with Max.

One large building on First Street stood out. Red brick, with an impressive row of white Greek columns. The State Capitol. Ready remembered with a smile how Pat Hull used to describe what the legislature did: *Undoing what was done last year and making laws to be repealed next year.*

He kept walking to the wharf, where he found a man selling steamship tickets.

"Excuse me, sir." Half-sure he'd be called a liar, Ready plunged ahead. "Yesterday, I left Oakland in a balloon...."

"You're the *balloon boy?*" the man exclaimed. "We thought you were dead!"

The agent shouted to a man mending a fishing net nearby. "It's the balloon boy. He's here. He's safe!"

The fisherman dropped his net and came running. "The balloon boy?"

Soon a dozen people had gathered. *How far did you go? How high did you fly? What did it look like up there? Were you afraid you would fall?*

"I'd be happy to tell you all about it," Ready said, "if first I could have some water."

"Water," the ticket agent called out. "Bring us water."

Someone handed him a flask of water, which Ready guzzled greedily. Someone else gave him a small loaf of bread. As he wolfed it down, the *Wilson G. Hunt* arrived from San Francisco, en route to Sacramento. The ticket agent shouted up to the people on deck. "It's the balloon boy! He's safe."

People streamed down the gangway and pelted Ready with questions. *How did you do it? We thought you were dead for sure. How far did you go?*

"Let me through," a deep voice boomed. "It was *my* balloon!"

Ready looked up to see Mr. Kelly pushing through the crowd.

"Glad you're in one piece, lad." The aeronaut grimaced. "Where's my balloon?"

Ready pointed wordlessly at the sky.

Soon, the passengers returned to the steamer, and the *Wilson G. Hunt* continued towards Sacramento. Mr. Kelly stayed behind and questioned Ready closely. Then the aeronaut filled in some details Ready hadn't known.

"That balloon was constructed to my specifications by the famous John Wise himself," Mr. Kelly said. "Wise said it was his finest balloon ever."

But something had happened on its passage from the eastern states, Mr. Kelly explained. Someone had thrust a knife into the folded balloon, tearing the silk in dozens of places. Though he'd spent weeks mending it, many tiny leaks had remained. That's why it had been so hard to inflate.

107

"Every penny I had went into that balloon." Mr. Kelly said mournfully. "I thought it the answer to my dreams. Instead, it was the end of them."

The aeronaut placed his hand on Ready's shoulder. "As soon as you took off, I followed on horseback as far as I could. I knew the balloon would lose its gas sooner or later. Unfortunately, I lost sight of you before you even reached Mount Diablo. Not knowing what else to do, I returned to San Francisco last night. Today, I took the steamer, planning to ask at every place if anyone had seen you. And here you are. Thank goodness for that."

Mr. Kelly wandered dejectedly away. The ticket agent treated Ready to dinner. When the *Antelope* arrived from Sacramento, en route to San Francisco, the agent personally escorted Ready on board and introduced him to the captain.

"Is there anything you require, young man?" the officer asked.

"One thing," Ready said. "Could I please have some paper and something to write with?"

The *Antelope* reached Long Wharf at eleven p.m. At a quarter past, Ready burst through the front door of the *Commercial Advertiser*. The editor, working on the next day's edition, looked up in astonishment.

"*Ready Gates.* You're not dead!"

Ready flashed him a grin. "No, sir, I'm not." From his pocket, he pulled out two pieces of paper covered with writing. "I have a business proposition for you."

A while later, Ready walked out of the newspaper office smiling broadly. The *Commercial Advertiser* had agreed to run an extra edition with his first-person account of the balloon ride. And the best part was, they'd furnish all copies to him in the morning. He'd be the only one in town selling his story. Why, he might earn more money tomorrow than he had all summer! He broke into a run and didn't stop until he got home.

CHAPTER SEVENTEEN

It was almost midnight when Ready bounded up the front steps and knocked loudly on the door. Horace Fitz answered it in his nightshirt. After staring at Ready with wide eyes, he called upstairs, "Mrs. Gates. It's your son. He's alive and in one piece!"

Ready's mother flew downstairs in her nightdress, as Hugh and Charles came out from their alcove off the kitchen. His mother grasped Ready's shoulders and wept. His brothers hugged him from each side. The other boarders crowded around. When his mother finally loosened her embrace, she pulled him upstairs to Father. Not wanting to hurt him, Ready gingerly touched Father's hand.

Mr. Gates closed his fingers around his son's and said huskily, "I told your mother that if anyone could get himself off that fool contraption alive, it would be you."

Everyone else crowded into the bedroom and began talking at once. Except for Father, they had all watched the balloon ascension from roofs and balconies, as had thousands of other people in San Francisco. But of course, no one had known Ready had been riding it.

That had changed when the ferries returned. News of Ready's peril had spread through the city like fire. Three people had informed the Gates family before Max could tell them himself. Monday morning's papers had printed detailed accounts, all fearing Ready was dead.

Now, everyone in the house wanted details. Ready talked until past two, when his mother shooed the others to bed. He stayed quietly with Father, until Mother returned with her Bible. She sat next to Ready, opened the book, and began to read softly: *If I ascend up into heaven, Thou art there …If I take the wings of the morning, and dwell in the uttermost parts of the sea, even there shall Thy hand lead me, and Thy right hand shall hold me.*

When she finished the passage, Ready kissed her goodnight and went downstairs to bed.

Tuesday morning, San Francisco hummed with the news of Ready's safe return. Every paper in town—including one in French and another in Spanish—trumpeted the good news. The *San Francisco Herald* called him a hero. The *Alta California* wrote, "His name will be spoken from Europe to Australia." The regular edition of the *Commercial Advertiser* gave brief details and advised readers to buy a copy of Ready's extra for "full particulars."

Everywhere Ready went, people surrounded him. *Aren't you the balloon boy? What was it like up there? Were you scared? Were you cold?* A French lady pinned a rose on his lapel. A German baker gave him fresh pastries. A Catholic nun in a black wimple told him, "I prayed for you, young man."

People thronged to buy his extras. If anyone asked a question without offering to pay, he smiled and said, "If you really want to know about it, why don't you buy a newspaper?"

By noon, Ready had sold every one—many for five dollars apiece—and pocketed four hundred dollars. He headed towards Winn's for a hearty meal.

A familiar voice boomed behind him. "Balloon boy! Master Gates!"

Ready turned around to see Doc Robinson, holding a copy of the newspaper. "Yes, sir?"

"Very interesting reading, young man. May I have a few moments of your time?"

"Of course," said Ready. "But I'm hungry. Can you talk to me while I eat?"

"I'll do better than that," the comedian answered. "I'll buy you lunch."

Over roast beef and potatoes, Ready regaled Doc Robinson with details of his adventure. Using his cap to represent the balloon's hoop, he showed precisely where he had sat and how he had tried to climb up the ropes.

The comedian listened intently, studying Ready's facial expressions and hand gestures. "Could you stand on the stage of San Francisco Hall tonight and tell the audience exactly what you just told me?"

The stage? Ready laughed. "Of course I could!"

Doc Robinson took out a paper covered with notes. "I was visiting with friends at a saloon last night, when someone announced the balloon boy had returned safely. This gave me an idea for a new sketch for my *Past, Present and Future of San Francisco*.

"I ran to the *Alta* office and got there before they'd started printing the morning paper. They allowed me to change my page-four theater announcement to include "Adams Express Balloon" as a new act. I originally thought to have Uncle Billy play a newsboy delivering papers by balloon, but I've changed my mind. What you just told me here is better than anything Billy and I could devise."

Doc Robinson's eyes gleamed. "I'll pay you one hundred dollars to be in my show tonight. What do you say?"

Ready laughed again. "Yes!"

Next, Ready headed towards the offices of the *Alta California* and the *Herald*. He was flattered by what they'd written, but annoyed by how much they'd gotten wrong. Their information was second-hand at best. He intended to set the record straight.

As he reached the plaza, he spotted Max loping down Kearny Street.

"Max!" Ready raced over to him. "What did you do with the oranges?"

Max's face lit up, and he gave Ready a light-hearted punch on the shoulder. "Until this morning, I feared you were dead, my friend. Is that all you care about—what happened to the oranges?"

Ready laughed and returned the punch. "It's nice to see you again, Max. Now, what happened to the oranges?"

"I sold 'em. I figured if you did come back and I *hadn't* sold 'em, you'd never speak to me again. I'll bring your share of the money 'round later today."

Ready wagged his finger at Max. "Every cent I'm due had better be there."

He went to both newspapers and convinced the editors to run corrected stories. As he left the plaza, he kept running into people who wanted to talk. He reached Lydia's boarding house by late afternoon.

113

"She's not here," Mrs. Salem told him. "She left shortly after noon and hasn't returned. Someone else came looking for her, too. Said it was a matter of great urgency. I don't know where she is."

Ready's mother said Lydia had stopped by the house after lunch. "I had just told her all about you, when Father called for me. When I came back downstairs, Lydia was gone. I haven't seen her since."

Ready had wanted Lydia to see him on stage. Well, he couldn't think about that now. He was due at San Francisco Hall in an hour.

Mid-way through *The Past, Present and Future of San Francisco*, a group of actors paraded onto the stage shouting: "The boy from the balloon—the boy from the balloon!" Then, Ready walked out to thunderous applause.

Doc Robinson joined him. "Lad, you took a ride on a rather high horse the other day."

At that cue, Ready recited his tale with gusto. Sometimes, Doc Robinson prompted him with an impertinent question or a joking remark. Ready would shoot back a sassy reply. More than once, laughter and applause drowned him out. He'd stand there smiling till the audience permitted him to go on.

Ready *liked* being on stage. Was this why Lola craved the limelight? Why Doc Robinson devoted his life to performing? By the end of his story, Ready felt a pang of regret because he didn't want to stop. But the laughter and applause brought him back to a feeling of triumph.

After several curtain calls, Ready bowed and walked briskly off stage. Lola had taught him the importance of a good exit. He left by the rear door, circled around to the theater's entrance, and slipped back inside. Then he tiptoed upstairs to watch the rest of the show from the balcony.

As the program drew to a close, Ready noticed a familiar hat down in the orchestra seats. Lydia had one like that. Could it be her? He couldn't tell from that vantage point. The man next to her was definitely not Horace Fitz, though Ready saw only the top of his head.

At the final curtain, Ready tried to make his way to the woman who might be Lydia. However, as people in the audience saw him, they stopped to shake his hand. *Excellent presentation, young man. You have a bright future ahead of you. Most folks would have panicked, but you kept a good head on your shoulders.* As much as he liked the compliments, he wanted to find Lydia. Finally, he spotted the hat, on the far side of the lobby's circular staircase and edged his way over to it.

"Ready!" Ignoring social propriety, Lydia threw her arms around him and kissed him on the cheek. "I was so scared for you Sunday night!"

"Lydia."

She squeezed his hand. "I have someone I want you to meet."

When the tall man standing next to Lydia turned towards him, Ready immediately saw his bent nose. "Joseph? Are you Joseph Peckham?"

Lydia's brother grinned down at Ready. "The same. I understand you've been looking for me."

"Let's get ice cream at Winn's," Lydia suggested. "I've wanted to show Joseph that place since I first saw it."

Hooking one hand on Ready's arm and the other on her brother's, Lydia walked between them.

"What worked?" Ready asked Joseph. "Did you see one of our ads?"

"You're not the only one with a story to tell," Lydia gleefully told Ready.

Mr. Winn greeted them at the door. "I have the privilege of serving San Francisco's boy hero twice in one day."

As Lydia had so many months before, Joseph gawked at the grand chandelier and the opulent furnishings. "Sissy Lid, what would Aunt Clarissa have said about *this*?"

"I can't wait any longer, Joseph," Ready said. "Tell me what happened!"

Joseph began his story. "I've been working with Hezekiah Waldow since late March," he said. "I met him in Marysville and we went all over. Spent a lot of time at camps along the Yuba River, following the north fork as high as Downieville. Then we dropped down to the middle fork, and finally, to the south fork. We went through Nevada City, Grass Valley, Iowa Hill. We meandered along the Bear River for a while, and the north fork of the American. I had arranged to meet the mail agent in Downieville in mid-May, but he never showed. We asked about him in other places and finally heard he'd been injured in a fire and all the letters were gone."

Joseph looked at his sister with a wistful smile. "My heart sank when I heard that. Lydia had been such a faithful correspondent, I knew there were letters from her. But I never dreamed she was in San Francisco.

"Hezekiah has been good to me. He's taught me everything he knows about daguerreotype portraits—the

116

equipment, the chemicals, how to achieve the best lighting. But he always wants to travel on the Sabbath! Since I worked for him, I had to do things his way. But I didn't like it. Not one bit.

"Finally, we pulled into Placerville on Saturday night. I told him, 'Hezekiah, tomorrow is Sunday and I'm going to church.' I heard Brother Brewster gave a mighty good sermon. So, I went and found myself a front-row seat. An enthusiastic sort, the preacher got pretty worked up about sin, and wickedness, and the evils of drink. Right in the middle of denouncing Satan in no uncertain terms, he suddenly stopped and pointed *right at me.*" Joseph demonstrated with his finger. "'You there, stand up!'

"I thought surely he was pointing at some one else, but he meant me. So, all embarrassed, I stood up. 'How tall are you?' he demanded. 'Six-foot five, Reverend,' I answered, all timid like a mouse. Then he says, 'How'd your nose get looking so funny like that?' "

Joseph laughed sheepishly. "I'm used to people making fun of my nose. But that's the first time it ever happened in the middle of church! So I said meekly, 'I broke it as a child, Reverend.'

"Then he said something that shocked me. 'Are you from Vermont, and do you have a sister named Lydia?' I started stammering. 'Yes, yes, why yes, I do.'

" 'Your sister is turning San Francisco topsy-turvy lookin' for you!' After the service, the preacher gave me Reverend Taylor's address and said Taylor would know how to find Lydia. Hezekiah advanced me money for stage fare to Sacramento and steamer passage to San Francisco. I reached Reverend Taylor's about noon today."

Joseph looked at Ready soberly. "I can't thank you enough for being such a good friend to my sister. When I think of all she went through just to get here and find me missing...."

Lydia interrupted him. "Reverend Taylor sent a messenger to Mrs. Salem's to find me. When I wasn't there, he tried your house. He arrived just after your mother went upstairs. I didn't even say good-bye. I ran all the way to the Taylor house, and there Joseph was!"

Tears rolled down Lydia's beaming face, and her voice came out in a choked whisper. "I could scarcely believe it. My two deepest prayers answered in a single day."

Joseph squeezed Lydia's hand. "We sat in Reverend Taylor's parlor and spent hours catching up."

"Come nightfall, Mrs. Taylor brought in tea and sandwiches," Lydia said. "Then she told us *you* were to be on stage tonight, Ready. We gulped our food and ran to the theater so we wouldn't miss a thing!"

The three sat in silence for a moment. Then Ready said, "Lydia, have you given Horace an answer?"

She studied the back of her hand, as her cheeks flushed pink. "Before I heard from Joseph, even before you'd left on your balloon ride, I told Horace I couldn't marry him. I'm only sixteen. I'm not ready to be a wife."

"I'm going to teach Lydia the daguerrian arts," Joseph said. "We're going to open a gallery in Marysville."

"We'll lodge with Miss Emily until we find our own place," Lydia said. "Then you can come visit us. And we'll come to San Francisco for supplies from time to time."

She took a piece of newsprint from her pocket and smoothed it against the table. "The *San Francisco Herald* says you're a hero, Ready, for holding on to that balloon and not letting go. But you were my hero long before that. When I despaired of finding Joseph, you held on to hope for me. When you promised to find him, you didn't let go, no matter how hopeless it seemed. You were my balloon, Ready, buoying me up when my spirits sagged. I'll miss you, but you've taught me a lesson I'll never forget."

"What lesson?"

Lydia laughed. "No matter which way the wind blows, hold on tight!"

Epilogue: Newspapers throughout the United States printed accounts of Ready's adventure, including the Philadelphia Ledger *from Ready's hometown. Even today, he is mentioned in a book published by the Smithsonian Institution called* The Eagle Aloft: Two Centuries of the Balloon in America.

It's unknown if Ready ever rode a balloon or performed on the stage again, because he fades from the historical record after September, 1853. Extensive searches of census records, city directories, and other sources of historical data have failed to turn up any mention of him in California, Pennsylvania, or elsewhere after that time. Did he stay out west? Return to the east? Fight in the Civil War? Live to be old or die young? Answers are shrouded in the mists of history.

More is known about other players in this story. Lola Montez and Pat Hull ended their marriage after a few months, but Lola stayed in the gold country for two years. Today, the house she owned holds the Grass Valley Chamber of Commerce. In 1855, she made a theatrical tour of Australia, returned to San Francisco in 1856, and then moved to New York. She died in 1861, and is buried in

Brooklyn. Her headstone lists the name she was given at birth in Ireland: Eliza Gilbert. Pat Hull died in California in 1857.

Doc Robinson produced shows in San Francisco for several more years, including periodic revivals of Who's Got the Countess? *In 1858, he left California to visit the east coast. He caught malaria while crossing the Isthmus and died.*

Reverend William Taylor stayed in San Francisco until 1856, and then returned to the east coast to write Seven Years' Street Preaching in San Francisco *and* California Life Illustrated. *Later, he did missionary work in Africa.*

Details of the sinking of the Independence *and the* Rassette House *fire are based on contemporary newspaper accounts.*

Although Lydia Peckham is fictional, her situation is not. During the Gold Rush, many women traveled to San Francisco expecting to meet fathers, brothers or husbands who never showed up. The problem was so acute, in 1853, San Franciscans founded "The Ladies' Protection and Relief Society," a charity that assisted stranded women for more than one hundred years.

Joseph Peckham's description of being snowbound in a cabin is drawn from a true account reported by Mrs. D.B. Bates, in her book Incidents on Land and Water, *published in 1857.*

The daguerreotypists mentioned in this book are fictional. However, "dag artists" explored the byways of California's gold region from 1849 on. Because of them, the California Gold Rush became the first major world event to be documented by photography.

ACKNOWLEDGEMENTS AND SOURCES

I first learned about the balloon adventure of Ready Gates from the book *Growing Up with California: A History of California's Children*, by John E. Baur. I then headed to the California State Library and other repositories to pore through microfilm copies of 1853 publications such as the *Daily Alta California*, the *San Francisco Herald*, the *Golden Era* and the *Commercial Advertiser*. Much of the detail of life in Ready's San Francisco is drawn from these sources.

I also consulted many books. Especially useful were *The Annals of San Francisco*, by Frank Soule and others; *Lola Montez: A Life*, by Bruce Seymour; *Seven Years Street Preaching in San Francisco*, by William Taylor; and *The Theater of the Golden Era in California*, by George R. McMinn, as well as various books and articles about Gold Rush-era photography by historian Peter Palmquist.

I am indebted to the research staffs at the California State Library, the Bancroft Library, and the Library of Congress. Archivist Lynn Bonfield also gave valuable assistance.

Thanks to Kendra Marcus, for professional advice freely given; to artist Jan Adkins for his beautiful cover; to my mother, Dorothy Lewis Kupcha, and to Carol Bohmbach, who both helped edit the manuscript. Much gratitude goes to Mary Bourguignon, Lynn Sadler and Shayma Hassouna for friendship and support. Special appreciation to my son Jeremy for computer assistance and general helpfulness; to my daughter Rachel, for always encouraging me; and to my husband Bob, who makes my heart soar as high as Ready's balloon.

Patty Reed's Doll: The Story of the Donner Party
by Rachel K. Laurgaard

In 1846, the Donner Party was stranded by heavy snows in the Sierra Nevada Mountains. The group endured bitter hardships and many died. But others survived, including eight-year-old Patty Reed. This is her story, told by her beloved Dolly, the tiny wooden doll she kept hidden in her dress. Pieced together from letters, journals and memoirs of Donner Party survivors.

ISBN 0-9617357-2-4 $9.95 Paperback

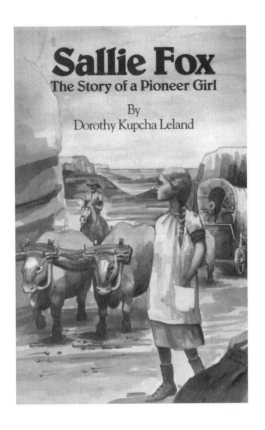

Sallie Fox: The Story of a Pioneer Girl
by Dorothy Kupcha Leland

In 1858, twelve-year-old Sallie and her family left Iowa by wagon train. They followed the Santa Fe Trail to New Mexico, then headed west. Suddenly, Indians attacked, stranding a hundred people in the searing desert. Sallie hovered near death. Yet, through grit, determination, and luck, Sallie and the others overcame the incredible odds against them. Based on a diary, memoirs and letters.

ISBN 0-9617357-6-7 $9.95 Paperback

Photo by Jones Custom Photography, Davis, CA

About the Author

Originally from southern California, Dorothy Kupcha Leland has lived in the greater Sacramento area for twenty-six years. She is the author of *Sallie Fox: The Story of a Pioneer Girl*, *A Short History of Sacramento*, and *The Big Tomato: A Guide to the Sacramento Region*.

In addition to her book projects, she has worked as a freelance writer, newspaper columnist, media consultant, and television news reporter. She and her husband Bob have two children.

Visit our website: www.tomatoenterprises.com
or e-mail us at info@tomatoenterprises.com